For

Kayleigh

GⲐDS

AND

mobsters

First Published, 2019

www.adammillard.co.uk

This book is dedicated to Niamh.

1

Our story begins, as many do, with a drunken fox playing chess with an angry squirrel in a dark alleyway. How the fox came to be drunk is another story entirely, involving a gallon of paint thinners, a blindfold, a weak resolve, and three other foxes with a dark sense of humour. And how this fox came to be playing chess with an angry squirrel is yet *another* story, which would, if someone were to write it down, take up more pages than it was worth, and so you'd be better off waiting for the audiobook.

"Are you allowed to move that thingy diagonally?" asked the fox, following some dubious shenanigans from the angry squirrel involving two pawns and a bishop.

"You callin' me a cheat?" asked the squirrel, slamming its paws down on the board, sending black and white pieces in all directions.

"I'm jusht not familiar with the rulesh," slurred the fox, trying to decide which one of the squirrels to look at, for there were three of them, each as angry as the last. The one in the middle was the least blurry, though, so it focussed on that one and hoped for the best.

"I'm over here," said the squirrel on the left.

Typical, thought the fox. "I'm not shure I should have shtaked my houshe on this game," it said, trying to replace its horsey, its castle, and the ones which looked like faceless children, the *prawns*, apparently. "I'm more of a... draughtsh player. Or dartsh. I'm... I'm pretty handy at backgammon, and... and..."

"You're pissing me off," said the angry squirrel, for it had had a really bad day, involving three of its brothers, a busy A-road, and the front fender of a Ford pickup. "Just make your move so I can go settle into my new house. Do you have air-con, by the way?"

The fox shook its head. "It's jusht a hole in the ground," it said. "Probably a bit of a downgrade for you. Very dark. Hot in the shummer, cold in the winter. Lotsh of shlugs, absholutely nothing in the way of nutsh. You wouldn't like it." It moved its King forward three spaces, then twice to the left, somersaulted it diagonally and right two spaces, and came to a stop just in front of the angry squirrel's Queen.

The angry squirrel frowned. "That's your go, is it?"

The drunk fox nodded. "Put that in your pipe and shmoke it," it said. "Or your e-shig, if you're one of them."

Now this only served to anger the squirrel further, and it was about to demonstrate its fury—possibly with a spinning back kick, depending on whether the sozzled fox remained still long enough—when all at once there was a blinding flash of light, accompanied by what could only be described as a thunderous crash. It could, of course, have been described in trillions of other ways, but none were as eloquent as 'thunderous crash'.

Three things happened in quick succession. Firstly—and luckily for the fox, who had no idea how close he had come to a walloping—the angry squirrel was incinerated, reunited with its three brothers far sooner than it had anticipated. And sooner than *they* had anticipated, too, for the trio had just purchased a nice three-bed tree in Heaven and would now have to convert the attic.

Secondly, the drunken fox sobered up in an instant.

An unexpected flash of white light accompanied by a booming clatter[1] will do that to a person, fox or otherwise. Not only did it sober up in record time, it flew across the alleyway and landed in a bin, as foxes are wont to do upon occasion.

The third, and perhaps most improbable, thing to happen would be talked about for years to come. It would be added to the curriculum in schools across the country. People would have an extra day off, thanks to the generosity of the Queen, and a museum would be erected in honour of the event, such was its notoriety. At least, all of that *would* have happened had anyone been around to witness it. Unfortunately, the fox would never be able to tell another soul, for its mouth had been permanently fused shut by all the magic and electricity knocking about the alleyway.

Still, let's pretend, for the purposes of this narrative, someone was there to witness it.

A young girl, no older than twelve and wearing the unmistakeable uniform of the Girl Guides, fell from the sky. Came through the blinding white light and the

---

[1] See? Not that difficult, is it?

deafening clamour[1], she did, and landed with a meaty thump in the middle of the alleyway, cracking the concrete and gifting the council at least six more months of overtime.

She lay there for a while, motionless, while the dust settled and the sky returned to its normal colour. The fox tried to call for help, but we all know how that went.

Then, the girl stirred. She moaned and groaned. She said something in Ancient Greek that would have had Mary Whitehouse spinning in her grave[2], and then she was up on her feet, knocking dust from her dress and sighing plaintively. For a moment she stood there, looking around the dark alley, ignoring the strange furry thing smoking at her feet and clutching what appeared to be a white castle. "So, this is it," she said. "Earth. No wonder humans are so miserable."

It was, the fox thought as it clambered out of the

---

[1] Last one, I promise.

[2] Mary Whitehouse allegedly studied Ancient Greek in 1969, on the proviso that Professor Stavropoulos took out all the bad language and violent words, such as kick, punch, and sodomise.

bin and crawled behind a bush, a very strange thing for a twelve-year-old girl to say. The fox suddenly wished it hadn't sobered up at all, for things like this are altogether more enjoyable if you don't remember them in the morning.

The Girl Guide frowned. And, as she turned around, the fox noticed that, strapped to her back, there was a nifty looking bow and a quiver of arrows. She was, the fox thought, one of two things. A) The kind of Girl Guide who you always said yes to, whether you could manage another box of thin mints or not, or B) not a Girl Guide at all, but a wolf in Girl Guide's clothing, in which case it was a very convincing costume, if you disregarded the lethal weapon attached to her back.

"Who goes there?" said the girl. And, in a flash, she not only had the bow from her back, but had it loaded and was in the middle of eating something which looked and smelled a lot like a barbecued squirrel.

The fox, sensing its days were numbered, decided that honesty was the best policy. It stepped from behind the bush, forelimbs raised to signify surrender. It tried to say, "I surrender," and that was when it realised its mouth had been unceremoniously welded shut. Now it was thinking of other things—such as *How am I going to eat?* and *What if I have a stuffy nose?* —but the arrow pointed toward it quickly dispelled those thoughts and the fox went back to shitting itself.

"One more step and I'll shoot," said the Girl Guide, and she meant it. She had that look about her face. "What manner of creature are you?" Now she looked intrigued, but only because she liked to know the name of the things she ate.

The fox shrugged, which is a remarkable thing for a fox to do, especially with its forelimbs in the air.

"Too good to speak to me, huh?" said the Girl Guide, drawing the arrow back. The bowstring creaked, and the fox made a little noise of its own.

"MMMMMMMM! MMMM! HMMM!" said the fox, panic-stricken. "HHMMM! MMMM! HMHMHM! HM—"

The Girl Guide was having none of it and released the arrow, for if there was one thing she couldn't stand it was arrogant fauna.

A mile away—as the crow flies, if said crow has a gammy wing and asthma—a dancefloor teeming with inebriated whippersnappers was positively bouncing. You couldn't move for lecherous twenty-somethings, sucking the necks of anyone unfortunate enough to brush against them and stopping occasionally to bump and grind to the beat of the music. It was the kind of place you wouldn't take your granny to, not unless you wanted her to replace your granddad and mess up the nice family-tree poster you had printed three Christmases ago.

The club was called SPINELLI'S, which was fortunate as that was also the name of the man who owned the joint.

Jack Spinelli sat up in the VIP area, flanked by goons and staring at any empty chair, a chair which would shortly be filled.

"Can I get you anything, Mr Spinelli?" asked the new girl, approaching the VIP area as if it were a crocodile enclosure and she was just a complex framework of bones and organs wrapped in meat[1].

"Champagne," Spinelli said, lighting a huge cigar. "Two glasses."

The barmaid went off—which none of them had expected, since her use-by-date wasn't until Friday—and then she went to fetch Spinelli a bottle of champagne and two glasses. On her way to the bar, she passed a man, bloodied and beaten, being held up by two of Spinelli's goons. They dragged him across the dancefloor, stopping occasionally to suck a couple of necks, and then on to the VIP area, where Jack Spinelli was rubbing his hands together and grinning.

"About time!" said Spinelli, chomping on his cigar. "I wasn't sure you were going to show. 'That lousy piece of good for nothing something-or-other isn't gonna show' I thought, but then I remembered that you owe me a lot of fricking money, and I thought, 'Of course he's gonna show. What kind of fricking sock-

---

[1] No one had told her this was the case. Ignorance, as they say, is Bliss, which was also the new barmaid's name, funnily enough.

sucker[1] doesn't pay up on time, especially when you were good enough to loan them the fricking money in the first place?'. You're a decent man, Vinnie. Do the right thing and start counting out my fricking money."

The bloodied and beaten man was unceremoniously dumped at Spinelli's feet, and the goons who had carried him in took a step back, blocking off the VIP area with their substantial backs.

"I... I don't... have it, Jack," Vinnie said, drooling blood all over Spinelli's designer brogues.

"You don't have it?" Spinelli said to the man. "He doesn't have it!" he said to the four goons standing in the VIP area, far more cheerfully than it warranted.

"I can get it!" Vinnie said. "I just need a couple more days."

"You know I can't give you a couple more days, Vinnie," Spinelli said, grinding the cigar out on his own arm. "Ouch!" he said, and then he hissed for a while, which is about the correct response to having a cigar extinguished on your arm, regardless of reputation or

---

[1] There is nothing worse, according to Spinelli, than a man who sucks socks.

stature. After three minutes—in which time the barmaid returned with champagne, two glasses, and was quickly redirected back to the bat to fetch a plaster for Mr Spinelli—the old gangster got to his feet and began pacing back and forth across the VIP area. Vinnie thought it was an intimidation tactic, but the truth of the matter was, Spinelli hadn't been to the toilet since lunchtime.

"If I give you a couple more days," Spinelli said, "then word'll get out, and everyone will want a couple more days. Before you know it, I'm sucking socks in an alleyway[1] just to make ends meet."

The four goons present—whose names are not important, not even to their mothers—stifled sniggers. They soon stopped, however, when Spinelli clobbered poor Vinnie on the head.

"Ouch!" said Vinnie, which was an appropriate reaction to being clobbered on the head. If he'd said, "Yippee!" he would have looked a compete tool.

"I can't see any money," Spinelli said through a

_____

[1] Not the easiest way to wash socks, but there's a fetish out there for everyone.

thick fug of cigar smoke.

Rubbing at the egg forming upon his bonce, Vinnie said, "That's because I don't have it, Jack. If I took out a wad of notes right now" —Spinelli began to get very excited indeed— "and started to count them" —and now he was positively ecstatic— "they would be counterfeit ones, and you wouldn't be very happy about that, would you?"

Spinelli deflated. Like a helium balloon with a hole in its arse end. "I suppose I wouldn't," he said. "Pick a finger."

This was a game Vinnie was not familiar with, and so quickly thrust out his middle one, which only infuriated Spinelli further.

"This is going to hurt me far more than it's going to hurt you," Spinelli said, and with that he produced a cigar cutter from his jacket pocket.

Vinnie quickly switched fingers. He could do without his pinky, but the middle finger was useful, and not a day went by that he didn't use it on some numbskull. "I would like to know," he said, "how this is going to hurt you far more than it'll hurt me."

"I might have exaggerated a little," said Spinelli. "Grab him, boys."

And the boys, whose names mattered not one jot not even to their mothers, grabbed Vinnie and held him in place.

"You have until noon tomorrow," Spinelli said as he slowly slid the cigar cutter over Vinnie's pinky finger. "Otherwise, I'm going to take the whole hand."

Snip!

Vinnie screamed. He screamed so loud that the people sucking necks on the dancefloor almost heard him. And when he was done screaming, he passed out.

"Someone get me another plaster," Spinelli said, wiping blood from his cigar cutter with a monogrammed handkerchief[1]. "This one's come off already."

---

[1] Spinelli's full name is Jack Leviticus Spinelli, which makes his initials JLS. To avoid being sued by Sony Records, on account of sharing initials with a well-known boyband, Spinelli's handkerchiefs are monogrammed with the part of London he now ruled (East) and how old he was when he collected his first debt (17). Clearly, he hadn't thought it through.

3

In a dark alley a mile away—by now time the asthmatic crow had run out of puff and had taken to shitting on parked cars instead—the fox could not believe it was still alive. It stood there for a moment, checking for exit wounds and expecting to drop down dead at any second, and when it found none, it turned back to the Girl Guide and said, "Hmmm?"

"I wasn't aiming for you," said the girl. "I was aiming for him." She pointed toward the opposite end of the alleyway, to where a man—dressed in a long white robe and clutching what appeared to be a giant fork but which was, in fact, a three-pronged trident—staggered back and forth, tugging at the arrow jutting from his shoulder.

"Artemis!" the man with the big fork cried. "What hath thou done?"

The girl rolled up her sleeves and marched across the alley toward the man. "You don't have to talk like that any longer, Poseidon," she said. "We're on Earth, Present Day." She yanked the arrow out of his shoulder.

The fox took this opportunity to faint, and when it

came to, both the Girl Guide and the man with the big fork were gone. But there, sellotaped to the fox's chest, was a note, upon which had been scribbled a few words in what appeared to be squirrel ashes.

DON'T TELL ANYONE YOU SAW US...

Which was, the fox thought, about as funny as a fart in a spacesuit.

*

In another part of the city, one far more noir-tinged than the nightclub scene or the bit with the fox, stands a tall building. It is not the only tall building in that part of the city, but it is the only one with the office of a Private Investigator in it. It also has working drinks fountains, a vending machine which only dispenses when it feels like it, and at least one flushable toilet.

Simian Knight PI[1] stood at his window, the moonlight hitting the blinds before it hit his face, casting that nice slatted shadow synonymous with the hardboiled detective genre. Any minute now, Simian thought, and a beautiful blonde dame is gonna come

---

[1] Not the cheapest P.I. in the city, but he's got a lot of 3-star reviews on YELP.

walking into my office. She's going to need my help to catch her husband in the act of adultery, and, after a few days of being in my company, she's going to fall madly in love with me, and we'll smoke cigarettes together and this dark noir world of mine is going to suddenly fill with colour, at least until she gets shot in the face by a red-head, who will then fall madly in love with me, and so on and so forth.

It was tough, being a private investigator. Tough and dangerous. Dangerous because of all the cigarettes you had to smoke a day. Dangerous because the traffic lights were all in shades of noir, which meant there was a very real chance you'd get knocked down, if you weren't careful. Dangerous because the women all wanted to either kill you, or sleep with you, usually both at the same time. The number of times Simian had awoken to find a broad looming over him with a telephone directory in her hand... well, it was just the once, but once had been enough, and Simian had taken to storing phone numbers on his mobile to prevent it from happening again.

Above all else, it was dangerous being a PI because

you always got asked to do dangerous things, things that the person doing the asking wouldn't do themselves, hence the reason why they were always willing to part with large sums of money[1]. When a really dangerous case came in, and after the client had left and Simian had finished crying into his "Best PI in the World" coffee mug, Simian often asked himself, "Why, Simian? Why? Why do you do this extremely dangerous job that no one else wants to do?". Then he would look at the cheque the client had left, see all those lovely zeroes scribbled there, and remember quite clearly the answer.

The *money* was why he did it.

He needed the money to take all the lovely dames out to dinner and the pictures, and then he needed it even more to pay for their funerals when they got shot in the face by rival red-heads.

Simian opened a window, sniffed the city air, then quickly closed the window, nailed three planks of wood over it, and tried to put the whole unpleasant occurrence behind him.

---

[1] And sometimes fish.

Suddenly, there was an urgent knock at the door[1], and Simian poured himself a glass of whiskey before answering, lest the potential client assume he wasn't serious about his job as a hard-drinking, heavy-smoking, hardboiled PI in a chiffon trench-coat[2]. He lit a cigarette, wafted the smoke about the place a bit, then took his seat at the desk. "Enter," he said.

When the dame entered, Simian couldn't make her out at first, for he'd gone a little mad with the cigarette smoke. But when it cleared, he saw her standing there, framed by the light seeping into the office from the hallway. If this were a cartoon, his eyes would have turned to love-hearts and popped out of his face, but it wasn't, so Simian did the next best thing and invited her to take a seat.

"Take a seat," he said. And also, "And close the door, would you? That light's playing merry hell with my eyes."

---

[1] As opposed to the slow, deliberate knock favoured by sloths and drunks.

[2] His regular PI trench-coat was at the dry-cleaners.

The dame without a name[1] shut the door, walked sultrily across the office, and plonked herself down, which was a shame as the chair she had been prompted to sit on was at the centre of the room, for Simian had used it earlier to stand on while he changed a light-bulb.

"Bugger!" Simian said, leaping to his feet and rushing around the desk to help the crippled woman up. Fortunately, she was gifted in the derriere region, and her fall had been cushioned somewhat as a result. Still, from what Simian could make out of her in the dark, she didn't look happy.

"Why's it so damn dark in here?" said the dame as Simian grabbed the chair from the centre of the room and guided her onto it.

"It's *noir*," Simian said.

"It's bloody *dark*, is what it is," said the dame. "Do you mind putting the light on?"

After some umming and ahhing, Simian put the light on. "New bulb," he said, motioning to the light

---

[1] There won't be much poetry in this book, but when there is it'll be just as good as this, if not worse.

fitting. The dame did not look as impressed as he thought she might. What she did look, however, now that Simian could see her properly, was beautiful. He was pleased to find she wasn't a red-head; long blonde hair cascaded down her back like a yellow waterfall[1], and she wore a glittery red dress which covered all the rude parts, just about.

"What can I do for you?" Simian asked as he settled back into his seat. The room suddenly seemed too bright, and not at all noir.

"Why are you squinting like that?" asked the dame.

"I think it's a 100 watt," he replied, once again motioning to the light fitting. "Anything over 40 is too bright for noir. Must have picked up the wrong one at the supermarket."

"At the supermarket, huh?" said the dame. "That doesn't sound very noir."

She had, Simian thought reluctantly, a very good point. It was time to change the subject and hope she

---

[1] Before you say, "Yellow waterfall? Don't be such a tit," it does exist, It's in China. It is the third most visited tourist attraction, after The Eunuch Museum and a skyscraper shaped like a pair of boxer shorts.

didn't notice.

"What brings a pretty lady like you to my office at this time of night?" There we go, he thought. Right back on track.

"I heard you were the best PI in the city," she said, lighting her own cigarette.

"I'm not the best," Simian said, "but I'm certainly not the cheapest." Something didn't sound right about that, so he had another go. "What I meant to say was, I'm certainly not the cheapest, but you get what you pay for, or something." He was floundering, so he knocked his whiskey back and shut the hell up.

"Well," said the dame. "I want you to tail my husband."

"Doing the dirty, is he?" Simian asked. "Having some how's your father with another sort? Bumping uglies with a lady of the night, is he? Having sex, and all that…. nonsense?"

The dame nodded, and then the inevitable happened. She burst into tears. "Oh, it's horrible!" she sobbed. Simian pulled open his desk drawer and took out the tissue box he kept there. This was the fourth box this week; he was considering switching to hankies, but health and safety kept fighting him on it. As he handed her the box, she snatched out a tissue and went on. "I just know he's up to something... I can smell it on him when he comes home..."

"Perfume?" Simian ventured.

"Fish and chips," the dame said, blowing her nose into the tissue. "There's some dolly bird started down at Harry Ramsden's."

Simian knew exactly who she was talking about; he had order six battered squid rings and a cone of chips off her on Friday. The dame's husband certainly had good taste in women. Anyone who throws in a slice of bread and butter free of charge is a catch in Simian's book.

"I want you to catch them at it," the dame said, and Simian noticed her demeanour had changed. She was now steely; the tears leaving slick tracks down her cheeks turned to ice and snapped off. Simian managed to catch one in his empty glass and poured himself three fingers of whiskey on top of it.

"I'll have to tail your husband for a few days,"

Simian said.

"That's fine," said the dame.

"And I feel I should tell you up front, I'll be very expensive and will probably spend a lot of the time flicking through *Dick Monthly*[1] and eating doughnuts in the back of my transit van."

"Seems fair."

"And I'll need to see a cheque up front. Something with lots of zeroes on, if you have it."

The dame reached into the clutch she was clutching and took out a chequebook. "Shall we call it ten-thousand up front, and then another ten-thousand when you catch them at it, so to speak?"

"Frnrfffhhhh?" Simian said. The dame must have been talking in pennies. Yes, that's what it was. There was no way she meant... twenty-thousand pounds? That would be a ridiculous sum of money. More than he made in six months. In fact, the last time he worked an adultery case he was paid in fish. Expensive fish, but

---

[1] Until 2011 it was called *Private Dick Monthly*, but after accidentally forgetting to put the *Private* on the cover for Issue 96, sales tripled. No one knows why.

fish all the same.

"I want proof," said the dame as she signed the cheque and slid it across the desk toward Simian. It got stuck in a puddle of tears on the way, but made it in the end. "Once I have proof, I can divorce that sonofabitch and take him to the cleaners."

Simian picked up the damp cheque, wrung it out a little, then stared down at it with some incredulity. Not because of the £10,000 only— scribbled right there in blue biro, but because of the name beneath it.

MRS STELLA SPINELLI

"That's funny!" Simian said, even though it probably wasn't. "You share a last name with the most vicious mobster in Stepney." He laughed, though none of it was voluntary. "What are the odds on that?"

"Pretty high considering I married him," said the dame.

"I was afraid you'd say that," said Simian, and he threw the cheque back at her. She caught it "I didn't touch that cheque, I don't know who you are, just go! Now! To think I was considering taking you to my noir boudoir[1]. Are you trying to get me whacked?"

"I'm not trying to… hang on a minute. What did you just say?"

"Whacked?"

"Before that."

"Noir boudoir?"

"I didn't know you spoke perfect French," said Stella. "However, I would never cheat on my husband, no matter how attractive I find you."

"Give me the cheque back," Simian said, "and I'll see what I can do." He didn't like this one bit, but the dame found him attractive and the cheque had a lot of zeroes in it. "But if he finds out about me, he's going to have me fed to the fish, or whatever it is he does to people who cross him—"

"Feeds them to the anteaters," Stella said. "Jack is terrified of fish. Says they look at him funny."

"Fish, anteaters, whatever! If I catch him at it with the dolly bird from Harry Ramsden's, thusly drawing a line under your marriage and splitting his

---

[1] This is one of the Frenchest things you can ever say. Try it.

considerable business gains[1] straight down the middle, he's gonna want revenge."

"Better keep your head down, then, hadn't you," Stella said, and with that she stood, extinguished her cigarette in the overspilling ashtray sitting on the desk, and turned for the door.

"How do I find you?" Simian blurted out in the most desperate voice imaginable. He might as well have rushed across the office, grabbed her round the neck, and suplexed her to the carpet.

Stella turned, blew him a little kiss—which he caught like a prize tool—and said, "Don't worry. I know where you are." She turned and left. The only proof she had ever been there was the cheque in Simian's trembling hand and the lipstick-stained cigarette butt in the ashtray.

Post-haste, Simian ate the cigarette butt and put the cheque in his safe, to which only he knew the

---

[1] Jack Spinelli owns most of the East End. What he doesn't own isn't worth owning, which is why the tanning salons and e-cig shops all go out of business after only a few days.

combination[1]. There was nothing to tie Stella Spinelli to him now, other than the uncashed cheque in the safe, where it would remain until he grew a pair big enough to take it to the bank.

After switching the light off and lowering the Venetian blinds, Simian dropped breathlessly into his seat. "What a dame!" he said, picking chewed tobacco from between his front teeth, rolling it into a ball, and flicking it across the room.

Dangerous business, being a PI. Especially when scorned dames are involved, which is pretty much every time.

---

[1] Most people use their date of birth for the combination to their safe. Not Simian Knight PI. He uses the Queen's date of birth. It usually takes him two attempts to get it right.

4

Many miles away from Simian Knight PI's office block, 1,766.9 to be exact, there stands a mountain, though it is not standing in the strictest sense of the word. Some people like to believe it is having a nice sit down, while others—madmen, usually—have convinced themselves that it is lying flat on its back, staring up at the stars because there's not much else to do. Whatever it's up to, the mountain is there, and that's really all that matters.

It is called Mount Olympus, and it's a bloody big bastard of a mountain, with 52 peaks[1], and upon one of these peaks, Pantheon, ten giant gods were gathered around a table, drinking wine and discussing important matters, which was a bit of a shame as it was getting in the way of Yahtzee night.

Zeus, the God of Sky and Thunder—and also King of the Gods, which he liked to remind everyone from

---

[1] Originally, there were only 51, but the gods on an adjacent mountain knocked up a conservatory, and Zeus was having none of it. The 52nd peak is not so much a peak as a UPVC porchway in which the gods keep their brollies and shit-encrusted walking boots.

time to time—tapped his thunderbolt on the table to silence the room, and it worked. "Thank you," he said. "We have matters of incredible import to discuss." He wished they were playing Yahtzee instead. "As you are all aware, as of this morning Artemis has gone AWOL." There were dissatisfied hisses and outraged mutterings all around the table; someone said something about rescheduling Yahtzee night to a week on Thursday. Zeus brought his thunderbolt down upon the table once more, and this time it fairly fizzled and lit up. Somewhere on earth, an entire flock of sheep, partially cooked, dropped down dead. "Silence!" he boomed. "The matter is being tended to as we speak. As you will all have noticed by now, Poseidon is absent from these proceedings."

Everyone looked around the table. Athena looked at Apollo, Apollo looked at Hestia, Hestia looked at Demeter and then Hermes, and Hermes looked at Aphrodite, Here, Ares, and Hephaestus just to speed the whole thing up.

"And we are to trust Poseidon to bring her back?" Demeter asked. "We all know how incredibly recalcitrant your daughter is, Zeus. It will not be easy."

Zeus didn't know how to take that, so he decided to pick at a chicken bone lodged between his teeth instead. "I'm afraid," he said, "we have no choice but to trust Poseidon. This is a family matter, which is why my brother has been sent to retrieve Artemis and return her to Olympus before she makes a mess of things, which I'm sure she will, if the opportunity presents itself."

"We are also her family, are we not?" asked Athena.

"I'm her bloody twin," Apollo said. "If anyone should have been sent to fetch her back, it should have been me. We've been wearing colour-matched clothes since the age of two. Been sleeping in the same bunkbed since six—"

"Silence!" Zeus said, this time staying his thunderbolt hand, for he had already reached his quota of dead things for the day and didn't want to have to put 50p in the overkill jar. "Poseidon has been sent, and Poseidon will prevail."

Hera reached across and took her husband-brother's[1] hand, which was a pity as there was a red-hot thunderbolt in it. Snatching her hand away, she said, "We must consider the possibility that Poseidon fails."

"Why?" Zeus said, fairly put out.

"Well… he might—"

"No be won't," Zeus said.

"But he might—"

"Hold my thunderbolt," Zeus said, thrusting it in the general direction of Ares. Ares took the proffered thunderbolt, for he'd been dying to get his hands on it for some time. It felt a lot more plasticky than he'd imagined, like one of those cheap swords you get from seaside giftshops.

"There is no need to get upset, Zeus," Hera said, in that way women do when there's a perfectly good reason to get upset. "I'm just saying we shouldn't put all our eggs in one basket, that's all."

Zeus snatched the thunderbolt from Ares' hand,

---

[1] Frowned upon, but perfectly legal on Olympus, where everyone had had everyone and to hell with the consequences and the freaky offspring.

and Ares cursed the gods, realised what he'd just done and quickly retracted the curse before it did too much damage.

"Eggs? Baskets? What are you talking about?" Zeus said, and now he stood, walked across the room to where, in the corner, there sat a water cooler. He reached down, only to discover a severe lack of cups. "Seriously!" he said. "How difficult is it? The God who takes the last cup refills the damn thing!" He brought the thunderbolt crashing down on the cooler, splitting it in two. Somewhere on earth, a dozen llama farmers fried in their boots, and another three were poached.

Hera held out the overkill jar, into which Zeus fed a 50p piece, cursing the day he'd ever suggested the bloody thing.

"I fear I cannot stand idly by while my siblings run amok down there." It was Ares, God of War and general force to be reckoned with, if you didn't mind losing. "I will go, Father. I will bring them both back—"

"You will do no such thing!" Zeus said. "You just want to go down there and start wars. I know your game, Ares. You're like a dog with two dicks[1], so long as you can fight someone for some reason."

"But, Father—"

"Your father is right!" Hera said as she settled back down to the table. "Earth presently has enough wars going on without you adding to the mix." She sighed and addressed everyone at the table, even Aphrodite, who had fallen asleep and was drooling onto an unmarked Yahtzee scorecard. "We have no choice but to trust Poseidon, and if he fails, well, we'll cross that bridge when we come to it."

"Then it is settled," Zeus said. "Now, who used the last cup in the water cooler?"

---

[1] From the saying, "He's as happy as a dog with two dicks," which is a fallacy. There was once a dog who had two dicks, but he was ugly as sin, and therefore one dick would have been one too many.

5

The streets were dark, and not only that but they stank to high heaven, too. In shop doorways, the filthy and disenchanted gathered dust as they slept fitfully. Men and women alike staggered drunkenly about the place. Some of them got into taxis, only to get back out again a few seconds later after realising they had spent all their money on booze.

Simian Knight PI had climbed into bed soon after Stella Spinelli departed his office, but after lying there with his eyes shut for ten minutes, had got back up, took a piss, washed his hands, took a second piss as there had been a bit trapped in the pipe, and then washed his hands a second time, before making his way to ground level and the dark, stinking streets outside and all around his building. It is there that we now find him, sticking to the shadows and, more often than not, the shadows sticking to him.

"Spare some change?" asked a homeless man from where he lay against The Bank of England building[1].

---

[1] It is a well-known fact that homeless people can take home, if they had one, as much as £40,000 a year if they sleep next

"I thought I was sticking to the shadows," Simian said, somewhat perplexed. "How could you possibly see me?"

"It's the chiffon trench-coat," the homeless man replied. "The streetlight bounces off it. You'd be much better off wearing a regular trench-coat if you're wanting to go unnoticed."

"It's at the dry-cleaners," Simian said, rifling around in his pocket for change. He tossed a few coins into the cup next to the homeless man.

"That was my tea," the homeless man said.

"Oh," said Simian, and, "Get yourself a fresh one." He placed another coin next to the homeless man's foot, and the homeless man lunged forward, seemingly alarmed. After snatching up the coin—which was only a ten-pence piece, for Simian was not made of money—the homeless man glanced up at Simian as if he'd never hated another human being in his life as much as he hated Simian in that moment.

"You killed Adam!" he said.

---

to a bank or building society, which is why you never see them buried in a sleeping bag outside Nando's.

"I did what now?"

"There!" said the homeless man, pointing toward something Simian could not make out. He could not make it out because it was dark and he was standing too far away. He leaned in, which seemed to make all the difference in the world.

And there, where there had been a coin a moment ago, Simian saw a crushed ant. Its legs were off in all directions, almost like a television antenna, and a tiny pool of blood blossomed out from its crushed body. Any moment now, two more ants would show up to carry it away, probably on a stretcher. Simian didn't have time to hang around waiting.

The homeless man was sobbing uncontrollably. "Cruel, cruel world!" he cried. "What have I done to deserve this? Isn't it enough that I'm homeless? Now you've taken Adam from me!"

"I don't think this is Adam," Simian said, picking up the ant and examining it closely. Two ants, who had just emerged from a crack in the pavement, one carrying a stretcher and the other testing a tiny can of Deep Heat out on its own face, turned around and went back down from whence they came.

"What do you mean, not Adam?" said the homeless man, still crying. "You wouldn't know Adam from... from *Adam*."

Simian had to do something to appease the homeless man, for he was drawing entirely too much attention to them. "No, this is definitely Gus Vans," he said. "I never forget a funny face, and this definitely the face of Gus Vans[1]. It's a little flatter than it used to be, but it's definitely him. Adam's alive and well! Rejoice, for it is a miracle!"

And now the homeless man did rejoice, for not only was he thirty pence better off, but his pet ant had not been crushed beneath the tattered soles of Simian Knight PI (or had, but he didn't need to know that).

Simian slipped away from the homeless man, stepped back into the shadows, where his chiffon trench-coat lit him up like a disco-ball, and headed across the city, camera tucked into his trench, making

---

[1] Gus Vans Ant was a legendary director of ant-based snuff films, such as "Daddy Wears a Size Ten" and, "This Doesn't Taste Like Sugar".

it look as though he had an unfortunate hernia.

Spinelli's club would be closing for the night, which meant the gangster would be off to see his mistress, before returning to the marital home, sweaty and redolent of cod and pickled eggs, for a second serving with Stella, if she was stupid enough to give him one, which Simian doubted.

Simian had barely made it to the end of the street when a voice from the shadows said, "Suck your socks, mate?"

It's going to be a long night, Simian thought.

"Just the one," he told the disembodied voice, quickly peeling his shoe off. "I've given most of my money to a bum."

*

Jack Spinelli exited his club the same way he usually did. Through the back door, wearing a Groucho Marx disguise, flanked by his favourite goons, neither of which he knew the names of, but they looked big and mean, which was good enough for him.

At the end of the back alley, he told the goons to go home, to get some rest, and make sure to give his love to their mothers.

"You had mine whacked last year, Mr Spinelli," one of the goons said.

"Did I!?" Spinelli said, far more cheerfully than he should have. "What for?"

"I believe," said the goon, "that she was," he paused for dramatic effect, "selling marijuana on your turf."

"Oh, that'll do it every time," Spinelli said, straightening his fake glasses and running his fingers through the fake moustache attached to them. "Can't have people muscling in on my business, now, can we?"

The goon nodded. "No, Mr Spinelli," he said, although he didn't look as though he agreed. He looked like a man who had watched his mother get whacked by one of his colleagues, and then had helped to dispose of the body in the only way Spinelli knew how.

Feeding it to the anteaters.

And if that wasn't bad enough, the goon whose mother had been whacked had been charged with the task of cleaning the anteaters out, which meant sifting through the digested and excreted remains of the woman who birthed him. It had been a particularly nasty Sunday, had that, for that poor goon, but it was all part of the job.

Or something.

"Well, off you go, boys," Spinelli said. "One of you has a mother to give my love to."

As they went, he thought about feeling guilty for a moment. He thought about it, decided he didn't much like the sound of it, and quickly thrust it from his mind. Once they were out of sight—which took a while, due to their considerable size—Spinelli turned upon his heels and skipped down the alley toward the street at the end.

"Suck your socks, Groucho?" said a voice from the shadows.

"Not tonight," Spinelli said without breaking stride. "Got me a hot date with a fish-and-chips vendor."

Through the streets he moved, stepping over snoozing hobos and inebriated party-goers as he went. Nothing, but nothing, could upset his mood tonight. It had been a great night at the club, and he had concluded some rather nasty business with Vinnie

'The Jockstrap' Aiello. Tomorrow, Vinnie would bring him the money he owed, and that, as they say in the trade[1], would be that.

After five minutes of skipping and whistling and rearranging his Groucho Marx disguise so that the moustache wasn't up near his eyebrows and the glasses weren't down by his chin, Spinelli arrived at Harry Ramsden's Fish and Chips, the best place to buy chips if you don't mind shelling out a bit extra or you fancy the new dolly bird recently employed there, which Spinelli did.

Margot Trix was looked delightful. A little coated in batter, and with fish bones stuck in her curly red hair, but delightful nonetheless, of you liked that sort of thing.

Spinelli liked that sort of thing a lot.

"Margot!" he said, pulling her into a tight embrace and pressing his lips against hers so hard, she would have to make an appointment with the dentist the

---

[1] Being a mobster (or mobstering, as it is more commonly known) is a trade, just like sweeping chimneys is a trade and painting over graffiti is a trade. Sucking socks, on the other hand, is a hobby, and a disgusting one at that.

following day. Also, the Groucho nose kept poking her in the eye. It wasn't the least romantic kiss ever[1], but it was close.

When finally Margot managed to prise the mobster off her, she said, "Phew," and also, "Ouch."

"You look beautiful!" Spinelli said, straightening his disguise for the umpteenth time. "Have you ever considered modelling?"

"And give up all *this*?" she said, motioning to the graffitied shutters behind her. Jack wasn't sure if he was being sarcastic, or if she really did enjoy frying fish in twelve-hour increments. "You said you weren't going to hide behind that mask anymore, Jack." She sounded disappointed, which was just the sound she had been going for.

Jack reached up and stroked the thick black moustache. "I did say that, didn't I?" He lowered his hand. "Well, you see, the thing is... inasmuch as... well, it's not really a big deal, but... and then there's the business to think of, and all that malarkey, and

---

[1] The least romantic kiss ever, according to the Guinness Book of Records 2017, was between a goat and an electric fence.

whatnot—"

"You're babbling, Jack," Margot said. "And not only that, but you're looking nervously around at the same time."

"Was I?" Spinelli said, looking around once more. "I hadn't noticed."

Margot was offended; Spinelli could see that. He had to think fast, say something to appease her, to make her want to stick it out with him, at least for the time being.

"Cheese!" he said. As appeasements went, it wasn't the greatest, but who doesn't like a bit of cheese, now and then?

"Cheese?" said Margot. She looked as if she didn't understand, which was just the look she had been going for. "Cheese, Jack?"

"Yes!" Spinelli said, and then, because of the way she was looking at him, he decided to elaborate. "Let's go back to the apartment. I've stocked the fridge with some of the finest cheeses known to man. Caciocavallo Podolico, Extra Old Bitto, White Stilton Gold... that one's got real gold bits in it, Beaufort D'Ete, Rogue

River Blue... that one's got real bits of river in it—"

Margot snatched her hand away, which was a silly thing to do as Spinelli was nowhere near it. "You think you can buy me, Jack, with all your fancy cheeses, and your posh champagnes?"

Spinelli didn't know what to say to that, but when he saw the unmitigated rage upon her face after he said, "Yes," he suddenly wished he'd taken a bit more time to come up with something better. "I mean," he went on, "that's what we do. Little fat mobsters like me, we get the trophy mistress by showering them with gifts. Did I mention the real gold bits in the cheese?"

"Are you ever going to leave her?" Margot said. "That bitch wife of yours?" That was, Spinelli thought, slightly unnecessary. Stella had never had a bad word to say about Margot, mainly because she didn't know about her, but still...

"Eventually," Spinelli said. "That is to say, when the right time presents itself."

"I can't wait forever, Jack," said Margot, running a hand through her chip-fat grease hair. "I'm not getting any younger."

"You should be grateful for that," Spinelli said, taking her by the hand. "Come on. Let's go back to the apartment, have a bit of how's your father and stare wistfully over the city. Did I mention the cheese has real gold bits in it?"

*

Two Minutes Earlier

Since the beginning of time, things have hidden in bushes. In the great Devonian[1] period, 419 million years ago, a species of millipede known as *Pneumodesmus newmani* (back then it was just called Dave) used to wait for days, months, even years before leaping out of a bush. It was all a complete waste of time, because *Pneumodesmus newmani* was the only land creature during that period, and therefore had nothing to hide from or jump out on. Still, it passed the time until the dinosaurs rocked up.

And now here, all these years later, we find a man hiding in a bush. It's a spiky bush, and the man hiding

---

[1] Research has led me to understand this has absolutely nothing to do with cream teas or pink-and-white nougat.

in it wishes it wasn't, but there hadn't been any other bushes for him to hide in.

"You going to jump out on something?" a tiny, high-pitched voice said, and when Simian Knight PI looked down, he saw a tiny millipede and was presently perplexed, for millipedes usually had gruff, booming voices.

"I'm on a stakeout," Simian told the millipede, whose name was Dave the MMMDCCCLXXXVMMMDCCCLXXXVIII[2]rd. "Any minute now, a little fat mobster is going to come and meet that beautiful dame. I just need to get a few pictures." He motioned to the camera hanging around his neck.

"Pervert," said the millipede, and then it leapt out of the bush, said, "Raaaargh!" and became suddenly frustrated when nothing happened.

Simian turned his attention back to the beautiful redhead pacing back and forth in front of Harry Ramsden's.

Why can't I meet a dame like that, he thought, and then he remembered that he had. Lots of times. They were all in prison, serving time for shooting blonde dames in the face. The trick was to meet one without a firearms license.

"Margot!" said a voice, and then Jack Spinelli stepped out of the shadows and kissed the redhead. It was, Simian thought, one of the least romantic kisses he had ever seen, and as a PI he had seen many. Had even been involved in a few. This one was especially unromantic, and Simian could barely watch, for he feared he was witnessing a murder. A really slow, sloppy murder with teeth.

Simian raised the camera and began snapping away. Yes! he thought. And also, Gotcha! He would have said other things along those lines but, out of nowhere, and arrow whistled through the wind and embedded itself, rather deeply, in his shoulder.

Simian Knight PI was not known for his manly screams, and this occasion was no different.

*

Two Minutes Earlier (Again)

Two gods are walking down the street, and one of them turns to the other and says, "How do you know

Adam was a Greek?"

"I don't know. How do you know Adam was a Greek?"

"Who else could stand beside a naked woman and be tempted by a fruit?"

Silence. Cliché tumbleweed moving from one side of the street to the other. Curtains close.

That didn't happen, but on *this* street, two Greek gods really *are* walking along. One of them has a bloody shoulder and is carrying a giant fork, and the other is in full Girl Guide garb. The one with the giant fork is trying to keep up with the girl, but she's fast. Like shit off a shovel[1].

"Artemis!" Poseidon said, wishing she'd slow down, for he had a right stitch in his side and his trident wasn't getting any lighter. "We can't be here. Your father sent me to bring you home."

---

[1] In the days when trains had a driver and turned up when they were meant to, drivers used to shit on the shovel and throw it on the fire as quick as possible. Because of the coal on the shovel, the shit didn't stick. Hence, "Like shit off a shovel." Unfortunately, it was the same shovel the drivers used to cook their breakfasts on, which explains why all the drivers died and the trains decided to stop giving a fuck.

"I'm not going home," Artemis said. "I'm going to live amongst the humans from now on. I'm going to change my name to Krystal, with a K, and find myself nice trailer-park. One with a nice tanned gardener who comes around twice a week to tend to the clematis."

Poseidon had never been able to find the clematis, let alone tend to it. "But you're disguised as a twelve-year-old girl," he reminded her. "And did not your father bestow you with eternal chastity?"

"Doesn't hurt to look," said Artemis, leaping up onto an industrial trashcan before dropping down the other side when it ran out beneath her feet. "I want to be amongst the humans," she said, "to enjoy life, and not spend eternity looking down upon them, judging them, making them do things under the pretence of free will."

"But you're a God!" Poseidon said. "That's what you're *supposed* to do."

"Supposed to do? *Supposed* to do? Uncle Poseidon, do you not ever wish you had been born differently? Lugging that trident around with you wherever you go, that's got to be a pain in the arse, and look at that big white beard! Don't you ever wonder what's going on under there?"

Poseidon shook his head. He didn't want to think about what was going on under his beard. Sometimes at night, usually when he was trying to read, he heard battles being fought beneath the hairs, and he was positive birds had begun nesting there. "I know what's under there," he said, shuddering. "And mind your own business." He shuddered again.

"I'm sick and tired of being a Greek goddess!" Artemis spat.

"Most humans would give their right arm to be a Greek goddess," Poseidon said. "They use it when they see someone of immense beauty. 'She looks like a Greek goddess,' they say.'"

"Then they've never seen a real one," Artemis said. "If it's not snakes in the hair, it's just plain ugliness. Have you seen Adikia? I've seen healthier looking faces on a pirate flag. No wonder Dike strangled her and beat her with a stick[1]!"

"If your father ever hears of your ungratefulness,"

---

[1] True story.

Poseidon said, "it is you who will be beaten with a stick. He will jam that thunderbolt so far up your jacksie, you'll be shitting sparks for eternity."

"Shhhh!" Artemis said.

"I will *not* shhhh!"

"No, shush!"

"That either!"

"Up there!" Artemis said, and she pointed toward two humans, mouth-fornicating in front of what appeared to be a Harry Ramsden's[1]. "Isn't it beautiful?"

Poseidon shook his head. So hard that several birds flew out of his beard. "It is not," he said. "In fact, that is one of the least romantic things I have ever seen in my immortal life. I have seen all the Tom Hanks films, I have read all the books about the shades of grey, and that is far less romantic than even those."

"Well, *I* think it's beautiful," Artemis said. "Look at the way she is trying to push him off. Such passion! Such—"

---

[1] There are three Harry Ramsden's on Mount Olympus, as well as a dozen Greggs, fifteen McDonald's, and more Starbucks than you can shake your thunderbolt at.

Poseidon was too busy upchucking to hear the rest of the sentence, which went something like this:

"Such love! And now they are arguing. Isn't that wonderful! Look at the way she is looking at him. It's as if she wants to punch him, and yet at the same time also mate with him. And now he is placating her with talk of cheese! And gold! There is gold right there in the cheese! True love at its finest! And I don't believe—though I might be mistaken, as I have on so many occasions before—they are even related in any way. True love between two people who, at one time, did not know each other! Imagine that!"

Poseidon imagined it, decided he didn't like the sound of it, and quickly thrust it from his mind. He straightened up, wiped off his trident with the hem of his robe, and looked about the place a bit.

In a formidable looking bush off to their left, he saw movement, and for an old guy his eyes still worked properly. He was extremely proud of his eyes. Good eyes, they were. Like brand new. And now, with his good eyes, he saw the movement in the bush off to their left, and said, "Artemis?"

She didn't answer, for she was still entranced by the lovey-dovey bickering going on out the front of Harry Ramsden's.

"Artemis?" he said again.

"What?" she said, seemingly annoyed.

Out of the corner of his mouth, which is the best way to talk if you don't want anyone else to know that you're talking, he said, "I do believe that there is a voyeur over in yonder bush."

"It's just a millipede," Artemis said. "A millipede going 'Raaaargh!', in fact. I wouldn't worry too much about it."

But, of course, Poseidon was worried about it. Not the millipede going 'Raaaargh!' but the thing still in the bush. "I believe there is a man in that bush," he said. "And that he has some sort of... *weapon* pointed at that disgusting couple." He could discern the glint of moonlight upon something, and that something was probably up to no good.

"I see him!" Artemis said, although she didn't say it out of the corner of her mouth, which placed them both in incredible danger.

"You must talk out of the corner of your mouth," Poseidon reminded her. "Otherwise he will know that we are talking about him and turn his weapon upon us."

"Right," said Artemis. And with that she drew an arrow from her quiver and prepared to fire[1]. "Bet you a thousand drachma I can make him scream, and not, like, a manly scream, but a really unmanly one."

Poseidon quickly checked his bank-balance, saw that it was empty, and said, "A thousand drachma it is, then," before crossing all his fingers and both his thumbs, a remarkable feat, even for a Greek God. "And if you miss, you return to Mount Olympus with me, and we put this whole nasty episode behind us."

Artemis smiled.

Artemis released the arrow.

Artemis grinned as the man in the bush screamed in the unmanliest manner a man had ever managed.

And then, all hell broke loose.

---

[1] It is technically impossible to 'fire' an arrow. Archers prefer the term 'shoot' or 'let the bloody thing fly!'.

6

Simian Knight PI had been shot at once before. Well, not technically shot at, but the bullet had gone past his head. Well, not really past his head, inasmuch as it went past his office building and embedded itself in someone's car. It didn't so much embed in the car as bounce off, as it was one of those foam bullets kids stuff in the end of play guns and run around going, "Da-da-da-da-da-da-da-da" with. But the whole unsavoury episode had unsettled Simian Knight PI so much that he became a recluse, took to drinking herbal tea and watching reruns of *Downton Abbey* until he dreamt of butlers.

He glanced down at the arrow sticking out of his shoulder and went, "Oooooh!" before his entire life flashed before his eyes.

Only it wasn't his entire life; it was more a highlight reel, the kind of thing you see after a half-decent boxing match, when all the spitting into buckets and prancing around the ring, not doing much, has been taken out, leaving only the really violent stuff.

And Simian Knight's entire life, with all the spitting

into buckets taken out, wasn't much to look at. Sure, with the right director—say, Steven Soderbergh or Lars von Trier—it would have probably pulled in good numbers at the box office, but as it was, it was certainly a flop.

Here he was eating ice-cream on a beach somewhere, sand-encrusted flip-flops protecting his feet from the copious amount of dog shits and rubber johnnies strewn across the seafront. There he was starting High School, or as he liked to call it back then, Big School, for the simple reason that he was still small, and therefore everything at Big School was big, including the lunches, and not excluding the lunchtime beatings from kids much bigger than him, with fists much bigger than his, leaving a wet patch in his pants much bigger than anyone had ever managed before in the history of school thrashings.

By the time that part had flashed before Simian's eyes—and it did so in excruciatingly super-slow motion—he'd fairly had enough and wanted the whole nauseating ordeal over with so he could get back to dying in a bush.

Unfortunately for him, God's a bit of a sort and wanted him to see what else he'd been up to in his life.

Here he was leaving school, and apparently at a time when it was fashionable to wear tartan trousers and comb your hair to one side, as if it's been raining, but only one side of your head. If he wasn't presently dying of an arrow wound in a bush, he would have been deeply embarrassed.

There he was smoking his first cigarette, for even in his tartan-trouser-listless-bouffant stage he already had illusions of becoming a private detective and had wanted to get the best possible start. Back then, though, he hadn't been able to stomach strong whiskey or scotch, and so had taken to sipping Tizer from a whiskey glass[1].

"How much longer is this bit going to go on for?" Simian asked, but he didn't think anyone was listening until the millipede popped its head back through the foliage and said, "That's a helluva nasty wound you've

---

[1] If you're thinking of drinking whiskey professionally, Tizer is a good way to condition the throat and stomach.
Alternatively, two teacups of Dr Pepper and just a dram of vinegar, and you'll be on your way in no time.

got there. Life flashing before your eyes, is it? Sorry. I'll leave you to it," before disappearing once again.

Here he was buying his first car. An old black Ford Capri with a red striped down both sides. Perfect for sliding across the bonnet like Starsky and Hutch, the Ford Capri, providing you didn't mind a little bump in the middle. The car had lasted him all of two weeks before the insurance company wrote it off, on account of all the damage done to the bonnet, as they pronounced in the documentation forwarded to Simian Knight, "Have you been sliding across the bonnet like Starsky and Hutch? Because it looks like you've been sliding across the bonnet like Starsky and Hutch. Over and over again. Day and night. For at least two weeks." That had been the end of the Ford Capri; his next car was a Vauxhall Velox, but its bonnet was useless for sliding across and he kept falling off it. Thankfully, this wasn't one of the bits which flashed before his eyes.

There he was, getting the keys to his office. The landlord, an affable chap, if you liked that sort of thing, had told Simian the rules of the tenancy, had warned him that the rent was extortionate but at least the building was shoddy, which at the time had confused Simian somewhat, but the landlord had shot him a look that said *Don't back out on me now, son, or I'll break your kneecaps and throw you in the Thames* and so Simian had taken the keys and scarpered.

Here he was taking on his first case. A beautiful dame, the first of many to step into his office[1] and write him a cheque which ensured he kept his kneecaps and didn't have to learn how to swim. Simian remembered her as if it were yesterday. Misty Forrest was her name. Dames always have names like that. If Simian had a quid every time a Misty Forrest or a Saoirse Minx or a Linda Hopeandglory waltzed into his office, well, he'd have three quid, because they seldom came back a second time, and often he'd have to chase after them on account of the cheque bouncing.

"Are we done with this bit?" Simian asked, for the pain was really starting to get to him and he had no

_____

[1] And after much negotiation, smoking, and whiskey, straight onto the mattress he kept in the store cupboard for opportunities exactly like this.

idea how much time had passed, and he wasn't quite sure about the whole 'life flashing before your eyes' thingy and how it worked in relation to time and space and relativity and infinity and so forth. For all he knew, he was lying there in a bush with an opportunist millipede trying to lever the wallet out of his jacket pocket.

Fortunately, that wasn't the case, for a second later Simian Knight PI, having witnessed a small fraction of his life—most of which was crap and didn't involve all the heroics he'd performed over the years[1]—returned to the land of the living.

That was when he saw Spinelli pull out what appeared to be a highly-illegal tommy-gun, turn in his general direction while at the same time pushing the beautiful redhead out of harm's way, and say, "Say hello to my leeetle friend!" which was a ridiculous thing to say, since it was a bloody big thing and incapable of reciprocating such feelings of sociability.

---

[1] He'd once, for instance, finished the local BIG BURGER CHALLENGE! Without breaking sweat, and has the certificate to prove it.

Simian fell back in the bush, and it wasn't until much later that he came around with a sore head, an even sorer arm, and a feeling of general despondency about the whole world.

*

As the arrow wedged itself deeply in the voyeur's arm, and he screamed out in the unmanliest manner imaginable, Artemis turned to Poseidon and said, "I don't think that thing he's holding is a weapon."

Poseidon shrugged. "It's a bit late now," he said, and it was because the man in the bush had gone into some sort of catatonic trance. "I think his whole life is flashing before his eyes."

Artemis felt guilty all of a sudden, for it wasn't in her nature to kill innocent creatures. Well, that wasn't entirely true. As the Goddess of the Moon and the Hunt, she was known for killing innocent creatures, but nothing ever in human form[1].

"*That* certainly looks like a weapon!" Poseidon

---

[1] She always turned men into deer before chasing them down with her handmaidens in tow, proving she wasn't a complete monster.

called out, and Artemis knew something was amiss because he hadn't talked out of the corner of his mouth.

Artemis turned and watched as the man who had, up until a moment ago, been tongue-deep in redhead pulled out what appeared to be some kind of futuristic missile dispenser and turn it on the man in the bush.

"Say hello to my leeetle friend!" the man said, which was a ridiculous thing to say as the weapon in his hands was bloody massive.

In that moment, time slowed down. If it had been raining, the drops would have fallen from the heavens with all the grace and speed of peacock feathers, or something. But it wasn't raining, so it didn't really matter.

Artemis drew another arrow from her quiver and prepared to shoot. Had it come to this on Earth? Were people just walking around in the dark with great big weapons of minimal destruction tucked into their waistbands, in case some pervert was watching from the bushes? Seems a little excessive, Artemis thought. And also, Not on my watch.

She released the arrow, watched as it flew through the air, listened to its gentle susurrations as it remained true throughout, heard the exclamation of, "Shit! There's a bloody arrow in my hand!" as it plunged into the little fat man's trigger finger, causing him to drop the great big weapon on the ground where it discharged one bullet, killing an opportunist millipede instantly and causing it to drop the wallet it was pilfering away from the man in the bush.

The redhead screamed, for the whole scene was like something out of a Quentin Tarantino movie, if Tarantino had decided to stop casting Samuel L. Jackson in roles and instead replaced him with a thieving millipede.

"Go!" Artemis said to Poseidon. "Make sure the pervert in the bush is okay. I shall deal with the other ones." And by the other ones, she meant the man staring down at the arrow in his hand as if it were some kind of camera trickery and the redhead effing and jeffing over all the blood dripping onto her Gianvito Boots.

"I will go to him," Poseidon said, "but once we are

done here, we must return to Pantheon, for Zeus is probably watching all this on his widescreen Dolby 5.1[1], and he's not going to be best impressed."

But Artemis was not listening, for she was too busy marching across the street to where the fat man was now trying, unsuccessfully, to yank the arrow from his hand. "I wouldn't do that, if I were you," she said. "It is tamponading the wound, and you will cause more damage by pulling it out."

"It'sh... it'sh thoing whathoothawoo?" The man could barely stand up straight, let alone string together a cohesive sentence. But through the drool and sweat, Artemis understood what he was saying.

"Tamponading. Preventing the blood from escaping."

"Like a tampon!" the redhead exclaimed, cheerily for some reason.

---

[1] It is commonly known that Zeus is a bit of a tech-addict, but no matter how much gadgetry evolves, you can always find him up in his quarters, cursing and blinding as he blows the dust out of a NES cartridge. According to Zeus, "What's the point in playing realistic-looking games? If I wanted to do that, I'd start a war, stand back, and watch the humans go at one another like in Call of Duty."

"Like a what?" Artemis said, before deciding she didn't truly care and turning matters back to the present. "You must go to someone who will remove it for you."

"Youthotme!" said the man, suddenly angry. "I got thot by a frickin' Girgide."

"He says he got shot by a frickin' Girl Guide," the redhead translated.

"I know what he said," said Artemis. "And I don't appreciate his tone. You're lucky I didn't put it through your head. What was all that nonsense about, anyway? The man in the bush is not armed."

"It's just a camera!" Poseidon yelled from the bush. He had the unconscious man wrapped around his neck like a stole. "I believe he was taking photographs of that disgusting couple from the safety of this here rosebush."

Artemis was surprised at how much this angered the man. So surprised was she that she almost choked on her own tongue. Had it not been for the spectacular set of tonsils at the back of her throat, she most likely would have.

"I wanthacamera!" said the man.

"He wants that camera," said the redhead.

"Well he can't bloody have it!" Artemis said. "I have no idea what a camera is, or what it is capable of, but it is not yours to have. It belongs to that man there, the one dribbling down the back of my Uncle, so unless you want a bit of fisticuffs to round off an already shit night, as far as you're concerned, less of the lip."

"Doyounothoolam?"

"Do you know thoo he hith," said the redhead, throwing an arm around the man, which he presently shrugged off.

"I don't *care* who he is," Artemis said. She turned, walked across to where the wallet lay on the ground, and picked it up. She opened the wallet, located the unconscious man's identification, and said, "Right. We'll be off."

"You're goingnothere," grunted the man with the arrow in his hand, for in the time it had taken Artemis to walk across to the wallet and pick it up, the man had snatched up his missile dispenser from the ground and was pointing it at her in a rather menacing fashion.

This was a man who meant business.

This was also a man who didn't know who he was messing with.

"You don't know who you're messing with," Artemis said.

"Oh, I know," said the man, and now he was doing that thing with the weapon where you're not quite sure who you should be pointing it at. It made sense to keep it trained on the big fella with all the muscles and the great white beard, for it was surely he who posed a threat, and not the twelve-year-old girl in the pretty blue uniform. "Ith'soo who doethn't knowooyouth methingith."

"Okay, can we just establish, right now, before this goes any further, that we are both aloof to whom we are messing with." Artemis thought about the arrows in her quiver, thought how lovely they would look sticking out of this man's torso, but a glance over to Poseidon told her everything she needed to know.

A sudden gust of wind gusted[1] through the street.

---

[1] Gusts tend to gust, breezes tend to breeze, and winds tend to do whatever the hell they like.

It came from seemingly nowhere, but it must have come from somewhere, since that's where things often come from. Something coming from nowhere, especially something as powerful as a gust, really has no place on Earth, which is pretty much where this thing came from.

Artemis braced herself, for she knew what was about to happen. Poseidon was flexing his muscles, and whenever that happened, things tended to fly around and about, defying the laws of all physics, and gravity especially, for they didn't call him Hurricane Sandy[1] for nothing.

The man with the missile-dispenser made a little squeak in his throat, which no one heard because of all the gusting going on around and about, but just because a tree falls in the forest, and there's no one there to hear it, does that mean it wasn't chopped down by a squirrel disguised as a lumberjack?[2]

---

[1] Not to his face, of course, but when his back is turned. They all had nicknames for each other. For years, Zeus has been referred to, by his closest nephew-cousins, as a Souped-Up Santa.

[2] Don't quote me on that.

The gust became a gale, and the man with the missile-dispenser was no longer pointing it at Artemis, but holding it aloft like some paramilitary Mary Poppins, as if he might start singing Supercalafragalisticputyourfuckinghandsup! at any moment.

The redhead was clinging onto the armed man for dear life, and yet Artemis was as unmoveable as ever, although her hair was dancing a little upon her bonce and her Girl Guide dress was fluttering about, giving her the appearance of an oversize Common Blue butterfly.

Artemis turned, and she saw that Poseidon's eyes had rolled up into his face, the way they sometimes did whenever he was using his powers. It never ceased to creep her out, however, and she quickly turned back around.

The gale was now a hurricane force wind. This was demonstrated perfectly, and somewhat cruelly, when a solemn-looking fox whipped from left to right, and then, as if once wasn't enough, left to right again. Artemis had a strange feeling she had met this creature before. Her suspicions were confirmed when the fox went past a third time and she saw the note— she'd recognise that handwriting anywhere, for it was hers, and had been hers since she was just a couple of centuries old—sellotaped to its chest.

The fox exited stage left, though not because it wanted to, and then all manner of detritus and debris began barrelling through the street. Trashcans, fast-food boxes... you couldn't see for chip-wrappers. All around now there was a howling, although some it might have been from a fox as it disappeared into the distance like an ambulance late for its tea-break.

No longer able to hold on to the missile-dispenser, the man let go, and the weapon whipped around a couple of times before being sucked up, up, up into space. Centuries from now, the spaceship Quazar Telebug III[1] would come across it, floating out in the endless vacuum of deep space. They would, using technology which doesn't yet exist, teleport it into the craft, and the Quazars would stare upon it with great

---

[1] The first two Quazar Telebugs crashed into one another playing space chicken.

fascination for a few moments before deciding it would make a rather nifty coat-hanger. But that is many years from now, and hardly worth mentioning.

The now-unarmed man and the redhead almost went the same way as the missile-dispenser, and would have had it not been for the lamppost to which they both now clung, span around, and generally jostled for position. The wind was so bad, a weather helicopter had appeared in the sky above, only to decide it was far too dangerous and not at all worth risking its life over, before disappearing into the distance, where a much safer occupation operating tours of the Grand Canyon awaited.

Artemis had decided enough was enough; Poseidon wasn't going to kill these poor mortals, had only been trying to make them see sense. She dropped down into a crouch, which as a twelve-year-old girl wasn't that far at all, and thrust upward with all her might, the bush-perv's wallet still clenched in her fist.

Poseidon must have watched her go, for the next thing he was flying beside her through the clouds—the unconscious man still wrapped around his shoulders like a novelty backpack—and was probably thinking exactly the same thing she was: it's a bit bloody nippy up here.

7

Zeus sat in his quarters, watching the whole thing unfold on his unnecessarily expensive and ridiculously whopping widescreen TV, and as he watched he thought things such as, "Nope," and, "Hoo dear!" He was missing the grand finale of *Masterchef* for this, which was bad enough, but the hurricane force winds generated by Poseidon had also played merry hell with his reception. What was the point of shelling out an extortionate amount of money on something that froze and pixelated whenever you farted too close to it? Back in his day, there had only been three channels, and they were black-and-white, and one of them only showed him a God's Eye view of the Earth; the other two channels were BBC Parliament and QVC[1].

"Hera!" Zeus called from the gigantic bed upon which he lounged in his Y-fronts and not much else. There was no point in being an immortal Greek God if you couldn't be comfortable while you were doing it.

---

[1] Zeus had once ordered a vegetable spiralizer only to receive a plastic shoe-rack in its place, but you get what you pay for, or in this case, you don't.

Hera entered from the en-suite bathroom, followed by a trail of steam and wearing a white towel upon her head. Upon her face was smeared some kind of mudpack. At least, Zeus hoped it was a mudpack, and not that he had to put in another embarrassing call to the plumber. "Yes, dear?" she said, removing the cucumbers from her eyes. She now looked like something racist jam manufacturers adopted as their mascot.

"You'll never believe what's going on down there?" Zeus was livid, and not only that but he was fuming along with it. His thunderbolt, which he kept in a glass of water on the bedside table[1], was glowing and thrumming and doing all sorts of things it shouldn't, not when it should have been getting a good night's sleep.

Hera peeled the towel from her head and began ruffling her hair with it, her words muffled as she said, "What's going on down there, dear?" she asked, in a manner which suggested she didn't really care, not in

---

[1] They say never mix electricity and water, but how else are you going to keep your thunderbolt cool on a balmy night?

the grand scheme of things, but that it was better to show she was interested, otherwise an argue would ensue and Zeus would storm off[1] out for the night to drown his sorrows and drink his body weight in Ouzo.

"They're only bloody fighting with the humans!" Zeus said, swinging his legs around and off the bed and poking his feet into a pair of fluffy Pegasus slippers. "I mean, I'm missing *Masterchef* for this—"

"Then why don't you switch it over?" Hera asked, for she was smart like that, as her Wikipedia entry can attest.

Zeus sighed. He sighed and he groaned, for he was grumpy like that, although there's nothing to say so in the scripture, as his Wikipedia entry is currently down due to some copyright infringement from a rapper in Detroit bearing the same name. "It's like watching those police chases, you know?" he said. "The ones where you know you shouldn't really be watching because it will almost certainly, without a shadow of a doubt, probably end in tragedy. And you know, as the car is hurtling through the streets at breakneck

---

[1] As he was wont to do, upon occasion.

speeds, and other cars are trying to get out of its way less they become part of the tragedy, and the police are maintaining a safe distance because they, above all else, especially don't want to become part of the tragedy, that you shouldn't be watching, but you do because there's nothing more refreshing than seeing a human making a run for it, and to hell with the consequences..."

"It's like that, is it dear?" Hera said, peeling the mudpack away. And now she was holding in her hand an exact replica of her face, minus the eyes and mouth, and Zeus had momentarily lost his train of thought, for the thing was so ghastly, so utterly and irrevocably disgusting, that he had to battle to keep his Horlicks down.

Hera sat down beside him on their God-size bed and said, "It is—" which was about as far as she got before Zeus interrupted her.

"Get rid of that thing, will you?" he said, motioning to the evil mask in her hand. "I know we have seen creatures beyond the humans' comprehension, beasts which would give Freddy Krueger nightmares, and immortal monsters whose mere appearance would turn a normal man's stomach, but that thing" —he poked a chubby old finger toward the mask— "is nauseating to the Nth degree."

His wife thrust the mask aside and sidled up next to him. "All I'm trying to say is that... well, let Artemis have her bit of fun. We were young once, too, you know."

Zeus pondered upon this for a moment, realised that he had pondered upon it for far too long, and said, "That is no excuse! Artemis is making us look like rank amateurs, and Poseidon is no better. He almost blew two humans to Kingdom come, wherever that is."

"Two humans?" Hera said. "From how many? In the time it took him to do that, four new humans have been granted the gift of life."

"So, what you're saying," said Zeus, picking up the TV remote and switching to *Masterchef* just in time to catch the desserts, "is that the humans are so insignificant that Artemis can do whatever she pleases, and the resultant body-count will not matter because the humans, even after all these years, have not grasped the concept of prophylactics?"

It was Hera's turn to sigh, although neither of them was really keeping count. "You must understand her frustration, Zeus. Up here, day-in, day-out. Sure, the views are spectacular, but, well... think of it like this— what's the point in looking at porn if you've got no knob."

Zeus shook his head, and the thunderbolt in the glass upon his bedside table did an excited little dance. "Not sure I understand that analogy at all," he said. "Do you want to have sex, or...?"

Hera patted him upon the head. It was a pat he recognised rather well, for he had shared a bed with her for centuries and you don't share a bed with someone and not know the meaning of a pat such as this. It was a pat that said, *Not tonight, dear.*

"Artemis wants to enjoy the Earth, and not only that, but probably the known universe—"

"Now you're talking bollocks!" Zeus said, for his Wikipedia entry, had it not been taken down, would have stated, quite firmly, he was a renowned potty-mouth. "Even I haven't seen the known Universe. Not even half of it! Remember that time I wanted to go to Jupiter, and you said—"

"It's too cold this time of year—"

"It's too cold this time of year," Zeus repeated, somewhat childishly. "Then there was that time the newspapers ran that special offer. Fifteen drachmas for two weeks in—"

"You wouldn't *like* Wolverhampton!" Hera said. "Even the people that live there don't like it! It's full of boorish brutes with red stripes painted across their faces, and that's just the women!"

"I'm not suggesting we go to Wolverhampton[1]," Zeus said, even though he had been at the time, and would probably throw his case into the back of the chariot now if he thought Hera was up for it. "I'm saying there are things out there even I have not seen, and I'm about as old as you can get before family members start shopping around for care homes and buying sporks because forks are just too dangerous and spoons don't work half as good if you can't keep

---

[1] For the people of Wolverhampton, I apologise. It's a lovely place to drive through on the way to anywhere else.

them the right way up."

"Artemis is just like you were," Hera said, and when the thunderbolt leapt out of the glass upon the bedside table and started danced spastically across the shag carpet like a beached fish, she decided to elaborate. "That's what worries you, isn't it? That she might make the same mistakes you did? That she could end up with twenty-odd kids, all from different cousin-brothers, and living on a run-down council estate in Stepney?"

The thought hadn't crossed his mind, but now it did. He couldn't help but picture her, not in the blue Girl Guide guise she assumed in her Earthly form, but a golden tracksuit with stripes down the sleeves and the word BAE written across its back, as if she were a champion runner and that was her name. He thought about that as the thunderbolt seared holes into the carpet and the television picture became no more than snow, and *Masterchef*'s dessert section was lost to him, and his wife squeezed his hand and squealed something about "...*burning down the mountain, you twat!* Or *not* burning down the mountain, for he couldn't really hear her over the sound of his infinite cells exploding within him like supernovae.

And then he came out of it, and said, "If she's not back on this mountain by this time tomorrow, I'll have no choice but to intercept. She my daughter, and as such she will respect the rules of this house, mountain, whatever, and that means doing what I say, when I say it, and not listening to My Chemical Romance[1] when she can't get her own way."

Hera, perhaps sensing Zeus was at his wit's end and deciding not to push her luck, began ruffling at her damp hair again with the towel. "Poseidon will have her back here by tomorrow," she said. "Just give him time."

Zeus stood. He stood and walked across to the other side of the room. At the other side of the room, he saw himself in the mirror and decided to throw a robe on. He threw a robe on and said, "I'm going for a little walk. Don't wait up." And with that, and a swish of his Godly robe, he marched from the room and slammed the door behind him.

A second later the door reopened and Zeus came

---

[1] Other lank-haired miserablist trendsetters are available.

through it. "Forgot my thunderbolt," he said, somewhat coyly. He picked it up, and it fairly sizzled in his hand, as it was wont to do whenever he picked it up.

"Where are you going?" Hera asked. "It is late. Why don't we watch Sinbad together? You *like* Sinbad—"

The sound of the door slamming cut her off mid-sentence, which was just fine as it had been a horrible sentence to begin with.

8

Greek gods are used to the finer things in life. Mount Olympus is what Heaven would be like, if you took away all the people floating about the place with glowing steering wheels hanging over their heads. It is impossible to walk down a winding path—of which there are many—on Olympus without some fella running up to you and popping a grape in your mouth, whether you like it or not. And you would often like it, because it would be the juiciest most delicious grape a complete stranger has ever popped in your mouth, and not one of those old bitter things the humans are forced to pay for at the local Asda, which they're only selling to clear some space in the stockroom for an incoming order of rotten cucumbers.

Oh, yes, the Greek gods have it made up there, halfway to space with their heads above the clouds, unless it's a particularly nasty day, in which case the clouds are up to your nethers and you can't see which way your legs are going.

Many of the gods have an entourage of beautiful non-gods, following them about the place and wafting them in the face with giant fans made of only the finest eagle feathers. Those not fanning the gods are busy watching them in awe, a pen in one hand and a souvenir from the gift shop in the other, hoping for an autograph to add to their ever-growing collection. You could get one-thousand drachma down at the local auction house for an original Zeus; fifteen-hundred if it's been scribbled on the back of a foam thunderbolt.

It is certainly a life worth living, which is fortunate if you're a Greek god as life never ends. It just goes on and on and on until the end of time[1]. And most gods appreciate all the special attention they get, for who doesn't like having strangers popping juicy grapes into your mouth when you're not looking?

But that is up on Mount Olympus, thousands upon thousands of miles away from the dingy, cluttered, and frankly uninhabitable office Artemis and Poseidon now find themselves. Never before had they seen such a state, and Artemis, as ever, eloquently said so.

"Bit of a fucking dive, innit?"

To which Poseidon, in all his Godly glory, replied,

---

[1] Much like The Big Bang Theory.

"Shit-hole. Complete and utter shit-hole."

The pervert with the arrow in his shoulder lay unconscious on the stained, brown leather sofa at one edge of the room. The other edges of the room were far too cluttered to drop an unconscious man.

"What now?" Artemis asked, for she was stumped.

Poseidon was flicking through a file-folder upon the unconscious man's desk. "I believe he is some sort of... private investigator," he said. "I wonder what that means." He looked up at Artemis just in time to see her flick a cockroach from her shoulder.

"I guess it means he investigates privates," she said, matter-of-factly. "Which would explain why he was hiding in a bush with that thing." She motioned to the camera sitting at one end of the desk. "It must be some kind of image duplication machine, specifically for use upon privates. Then, he brings the machine back here so that he can investigate them more closely. I'm starting to think we would have left him to die."

Poseidon walked around to the camera and picked it up, all the while clicking his tongue. "You really don't know what a camera is?" he said.

Artemis shook her head, which was the correct response because she hadn't the foggiest.

"It is used by the humans to capture perfect moments in time, those beautiful occurrences which only come around so often. They then print out the pictures and stick them in little hardbound books so they can stare upon them in fond remembrance whenever a distant relative comes around."

"This guy" —she motioned to the unconscious man on the sofa— "takes pictures of people's gonads and then shows them to his family? What a world these humans are making for themselves down here!"

"I do not believe," said Poseidon, "that this man was capturing pictures of that disgusting couple's privates. In fact, I'm not quite certain he is an investigator of privates at all."

"But you said—"

"It could mean many things," Poseidon interrupted, snatching his trident up from where it had been leaning against the desk. "For instance, it could mean that he is a..."

"A...?"

"An investigator who keeps himself to himself."

"That's just ridiculous," Artemis said. "He'd never get anything done."

"Or it could mean that he provides an investigating service to very private people."

"Nope," Artemis said. "I fear we are still a mile away with this."

"Perhaps he is, and this is the one I believe to be most feasible, a *gumshoe*." Poseidon said it with such fervour, such confidence, that it came as quite a shock when Artemis just shrugged.

"Perhaps he is!" she said with fake enthusiasm. "Or perhaps he is a wetbird or a cheesesock or a football... actually, forget that last one because it's a real thing, but the others aren't! You can't make up words and then call people them."

"Of *course* you can," Poseidon said, calmly. "People do it every day. And besides, gumshoe is a real word. Have you never read the works of Carroll John Daly? Dashiell Hammett? Raymond Chandler?"

Artemis had her hands to her face now and was squeezing it together, distorting her features. "Oh!

Have you never watched *Spiceworld: The Movie*?" Poseidon's frown told her that he hadn't, and also that he was one of the fortunate ones. "I don't know who those people are, or if they even exist."

"I can assure you that they did exist, and they created some of the best gumshoes ever committed to the page. And since this office is primarily black-and-white, and the unconscious man over there has had Venetian blinds fitted[1], one can safely assume that a private investigator is a gumshoe, and therefore the man drooling down his own sofa is a gumshoe, and that is that."

"So, he's a gumshoe," Artemis said, shrugging indifferently. "Let us all bathe in his splendour. What should we do about the fact that he is mortal, and therefore liable to bleed to death if we do not do something about the arrow sticking out of his shoulder?"

---

[1] The Venetian blinds in Simian Knight's office haven't always been there. Before that, there was a lovely bit of graffitied wood nailed to the window frame, which was either to keep the riff-raff out or in, depending on which way you were coming from.

The unconscious man groaned a little bit, popped his tongue out, did a weird twitching thing with his right eye, and then fell completely still again. As he performed this strange little combination of tics, grunts, and convulsions, Artemis and Poseidon tried to make themselves look as innocuous as possible, which involved a lot of pointing away at things that weren't there, sitting down upon the desk before standing back up again, and general shifting of position, lest the man suddenly come to and assume they were here to rob the place.

Poseidon walked toward the snoozing man, rubbing his hands together as if he were about to provide the most sensual massage ever experienced to a man who was too comatose to care. When he instead whipped out a small black box and thrust it to his own ear, it came as something of a surprise to Artemis, for she hadn't seen that model in years.

"Is that a $\pi\sum\prod$ [1]?" she asked, with more incredulity

---

[1] The $\pi\sum\prod$ is a decent way of communicating with other Greek gods at any given time, providing you're not in the Welsh mountains or going under a bridge. Poseidon's package includes fifty free texts, ten minutes of free calls,

than she had ever mustered before.

Suddenly embarrassed, and a little defensive, Poseidon said, "I'm not due an upgrade until next century. Long contract, and all that." He thrust a finger to his lips to silence Artemis—even though she hadn't been speaking, but her laughter was just as annoying—and said into the device, "Aceso."

The voice which came back was not of Aceso, but of her assistant, Trevor. "Hello? Aceso's office, how may I direct your call?"

Poseidon visibly deflated, for they were running out of time. "You can direct it directly to Aceso," he said, and hoped that was enough. Apparently, it was not.

"Aceso is currently having lunch with the King of Cambodia. It's a very important meeting, you see. Lots of people to heal in Cambodia, what with all the Dengue Fever and Malaria and whatnot, and the King wants to set up a standing order—"

"If you don't put Aceso on the $\pi\sum\prod$ in the next ten

---

and a monthly subscription to $\pi\sum\prod$ Magazine, whose circulation is one and has been for the past three-hundred years.

seconds, I will come over there and stick my trident so far up your—"

"Hello?" Aceso's voice came through the π∑∏, cutting Poseidon off mid-sentence, which was fortunate as it was turning out to be a rather offensive one.

"Aceso!" Poseidon said, taking her off speaker-π∑∏. "It's me, Poseidon. Yeah it has been a while, hasn't it? What? No, I'm not going through a tunnel. Wales? No, haven't been there in some millennia? Hang on a second." And with that he walked across to the other side of the dank office and said, "How about now? Oh, good. Yes, not too bad thanks. Been playing lots of chess lately, you know how it gets... yes, look, I didn't call to discuss the weather in Cambodia... I know it's bloody hot, that's why they put it in Cambodia and not Scotland... yes, if you would be so kind as to permit me to speak for a moment... yes, as a matter of fact something is very wrong... no, it is not syphilis... look, Aceso, I need your assistance with something. It is a matter of life and death... yes, I know that we are immortal. It is not a matter of *my* life and death... a human. In fact, a gumshoe in Stepney... actually I *have* read Raymond Chandler, and agree completely with your somewhat unsolicited opinion... as quick as you can, really. I would say he has less than" —he glanced over to the unconscious man drooling on the sofa— "five minutes. Ten if we turn the heating up a bit."

Artemis watched all this, fascinated. She had never met Aceso before, but it appeared she was about to, which was great news because there was a mole just between her bum-cheeks that she wanted a second opinion on.

"You'll be here in ten seconds?" Poseidon said with a smile. "That would be wonderful. Okay, see you in ten... no you hang up... you hang up... no *you*—" But then the π∑∏ was no longer in his hand as Artemis hung up and passed it back to him.

Poseidon had been in the process of formulating another nasty sentence, this time for Artemis, when a sudden golden light began to fizzle into existence at the centre of the office. It was the kind of light you ought to run away from, under most circumstances, as it meant one of three things. That there was a tear in the fabric of reality itself, in which case something interdimensional was about to come through it and cause mass destruction the likes of which humans hadn't seen since Miley Cyrus twerked herself silly at the MTV VMA's. That those white-coats over at CERN, the European Organisation for Nuclear Research[1], had finally recreated the big bang and now it had popped up in someone's grimy office block in Stepney. Or that a Greek goddess was about to manifest after being, without much ceremony, pulled out of a very important meeting with the King of Cambodia.

Artemis had her fingers crossed for the CERN outcome.

And was almost disappointed to find, a moment later, standing there where the golden light had been fizzling, was a generic-looking blonde beauty dressed in a white robe and with golden sandals upon perfectly-manicured feet. Which was fine, if you liked that sort of thing.

---

[1] An acronym that works on absolutely no level (unless you're French, in which case it works just fine) and if they can't get that right, then how can they be trusted with particle accelerators?

Poseidon clearly liked that sort of thing. "Aceso!" he said, rushing across the room to the goddess. "How lovely to see you again. What's it been? Ten, fifteen centuries?"

"More like twenty," she said, playfully jabbing him in the arm as if they were old mates and he had just told the best Your Mom joke ever. "How come you never call?"

"I only get ten minutes of free calls every century or so," he said, "and I'm not due an upgrade for—"

"Artemis," Aceso said, about as affectionless as one could say it without punctuating it with a headbutt.

Artemis bowed, for she definitely wanted the goddess to take a look at her little problem before she popped off back to Cambodia. "Aceso."

"So where is this human?" said Aceso, glancing about the place with a look of abject horror and biting her tongue as if she'd rather take it clean off than taste the air around her any longer than was necessary.

"He's right there," Poseidon said, and he pointed toward the unconscious man on the sofa.

"Oh!" Aceso said. "I almost didn't see him through

all the darkness. Why are there no lights in here, and I thought Venetian blinds were a thing of the past?"

"He's a—"

"Oh, yes, a gumshoe," Aceso said, as if it made perfect sense. She walked across the room to the human and dropped into a crouch beside him. "This looks nasty."

"Funny you should say that," Artemis said as she began to hike up her dress, for there was no time like the present[1]. It wasn't until Poseidon stuck his trident in her back that she realised it was, perhaps, better to wait until Aceso had saved the human.

"Who shot him with an arrow?" Aceso asked, fingering the arrow as if trying to decide the best course of action.

"I did," Artemis said. "But only because I thought he was a pervert."

"And he is *not* a pervert?" Aceso said, giving the arrow a little twist this way and that.

"He might be," Artemis said. "We haven't had a chance to ask him yet."

---

[1] If this is true, why were the eighties so much fun?

"Right, well, I'm going to have to yank it out and hope for the best," Aceso said, which was pretty much what Artemis was going to suggest. "I suggest you both take a step back. This could get rather messy, and if you rock up at the local Launderette with bloody robes" — she motioned to Poseidon in particular— "they're probably going to ask a few questions, but not until they've made a call to the gendarme."

Poseidon took a step back and, with a little coaxing, so did Artemis.

"Right!" Aceso said to the unconscious gumshoe. "Let's get this thing out of you."

She placed both hands upon the arrow, and the gumshoe groaned, and she gave it a little tug, and the gumshoe went, "Oooooh!" and then, with all her might—there was a lot of it, being a Greek goddess— she yanked the arrow upwards and—

The gumshoe bolted upright and said, "Ferfucksake!" which was about the correct response, and for a moment he seemed disorientated, glancing about the room, taking it all in, including the three strangers looking down upon him. "Who are—"

Poseidon clobbered him in the face and the gumshoe fell unconscious once again.

"What did you do that for?" Artemis asked, for it seemed a little unreasonable, a little over the top, and a lot uncalled for. She wasn't against violence, per se, but violence for the sake of violence, that she had an issue with.

"He cannot see us," Poseidon said, shaking his hand out in that way people do after they've just walloped something harder than their hand.

"He can't see *anything* now!" Artemis said. "I mean, I thought we were going to question him a bit, find out his game and all that?"

Aceso held her hand over the wound in the gumshoe's shoulder, and a great golden glow began to appear forthwith. "Poseidon is right," she said as she did whatever it was she was doing. "Mortals do not need to know about us."

"Says the woman who was, up until a moment ago, schmoozing with the King of Cambodia." Artemis couldn't get her head around this. It was a great big U-bend of a mystery. "I mean, what's the point of being a

Greek God if the humans don't know we exist. Maybe if they knew, they'd stop fannying around down here." She was passionate about the universe and most of the things in it, couldn't bear to see worlds destroyed just because Martha won't shell out an extra ten pence for a bag-for-life. No, the humans needed someone to look up to, someone from the history books, someone they could *all* believe in, and not just half the population who were deemed crazy by creationists.

"We do not interfere with the humans," Poseidon said, polishing his trident with the sleeve of his robe. "Let them go about their business. Their fates are not ours to decide."

"You weren't saying that when you were egging me on to put an arrow in this bush-whacker!" Artemis said, and she had a point. "Which, by the way, you owe me a thousand drachmas for."

Poseidon glanced about the office until he found something to distract Artemis with. "Is that real whiskey, I wonder," he said. "Sometimes, the humans drink Tizer as an alternative."

Artemis was having none of it, for she stood there

with her hand out, palm up, awaiting payment.

"Oh, you'll get your thousand drachmas as soon as we return to Mount Olympus," Poseidon said, and she lowered her hand, whispered something about Poseidon's mother and her popularity with sailors, and then turned her attention back to Aceso.

"Is this going to take long?" she asked. "Only it'll be morning soon, and I've yet to decide on where I'm going to take breakfast." Although she had passed something a little earlier professing to sell the biggest full-English in the country. 'So big you'll need a toilet break at the halfway point', apparently, which sounded great to Artemis as she was hungry enough to eat the backside off a low-flying duck. It really was amazing how much hungrier you were when you didn't have a complete stranger popping juicy grapes into your mouth every hundred yards.

"Almost done," said Aceso. "You can't rush the healing process," she added.

"But that's precisely what you're doing now," Artemis said, for the wound in the comatose gumshoe had not only stopped bleeding, but was now cauterised and on its way to disappearing altogether.

"What do you mean 'taking breakfast'?" Poseidon said, all at once confused and a little perturbed. "You are not taking breakfast anywhere on Earth, Artemis. We are going to return to Mount Olympus post-haste, and there you will receive the breakfast of the gods—"

"I've had it up to here with grapes!" Artemis said, demonstrating with her hand just how high it was that she had had it up to. "I want a proper breakfast. One that I have to take a toilet-break halfway through. I'm sick of lepers pushing fruit into my face. I want it on a nice floral-pattered plate, with a knife and fork and a little spoon for my teacup. Do you know how dangerous it is to let the non-gods feed us grapes all the time? It's a wonder we're not extinct."

"All done!" Aceso said, cheerily getting to her feet. "He should be right as rain in a few hours. An inch to the left and he would be brown bread by now."

"I want a slice of brown bread," Artemis went on, "with real butter, and I want some black pudding," and now she licked her lips, for she was drooling like a coke addict at an all-you-can-snort buffet, "and I want—"

"You're very welcome," Aceso said, sarcastically. "I'll be off then, shall I?"

"And I want a waitress whose name is something like Cilla or Becs or Wendy, and she'll have pink hair, but faded, like she started off with good intentions but then couldn't keep up with the maintenance—"

A golden aura wrapped itself around Aceso momentarily, and then she was gone.

"You're not going for breakfast on Earth!" Poseidon said, in that manner which suggests a decision is final.

Six hours later, he would be dipping a piece of toast into a runny egg and trying not to cry, but we'll cross that bridge when we come to it.

9

It is a well-known fact that if you don't want someone to know you're there, the chances of you being discovered increase significantly[1]. A drunk returns home, slips his key into the lock in what he deems to be silent, but is in fact noisier than a pack of stampeding wildebeest. Once inside he tiptoes up the stairs like a fireworks display, takes a piss on the bathroom floor like a riot squad's water cannon, and then proceeds to the bedroom like a New Year's Eve fireworks display, and is then shocked and surprised to find his wife sitting on the edge of the bed with a frown about her face and wielding a rolling pin like one of the seven samurai. It is the nature of things. So shall it be, forever and ever, amen.

Jack Spinelli was not drunk when he arrived back at the penthouse apartment he shared with his wife, Stella, but the same rules applied, which was why Stella met him at the door before he even had a foot through it.

---

[1] Just ask Wally (or Waldo, depending on which side of the globe you're currently sitting on).

"Good night at the club?" she asked, arms folded across her chest.

At least she's not wielding a rolling pin like one of the seven samurai, Spinelli thought. "Quiet," he said, easing past her. "Did you know I had one of my men's mothers whacked?"

"You might have mentioned it," Stella said as she shut the door and followed him into the large living room[1]. "Stop for fish-and-chips on the way home, did you?"

"You're not, by any chance, concealing a rolling pin upon your person, are you?" Spinelli asked.

"Answer the question."

"I was *going* to," he said, holding his hand up to reveal a bloodstained bandage, "but some pricks decided to shoot me with an arrow, which is why it is now," —he looked at his Rolex, saw that it was no longer working due to all the blood in its innards, and

---

[1] So large was this living room that you could have divided it up into studio apartments, filled it with students, and spent the rest of your days living on Mars with the rent profits. Why anyone would want to do that, though, is anyone's guess, which is why it is, and always will be, just a big living room.

made a mental note to pick up a new one in the morning— "well, I don't know, but the point is I've been at the fricking hospital for the past fricking three hours while some fricking junior doctor poked me with a fricking needle and asked me all sorts of questions about how I came to have a fricking arrow sticking in me."

Stella's demeanour seemed to soften then, and she rushed across the living room—it took her almost thirty seconds to reach him—and began examining the bandage as if she had, while Spinelli had been gone, taken a Medical Degree and passed with flying colours, which she hadn't and therefore didn't. "Ooooh!" she said, and then, "How did this happen? Who fires an arrow at someone?"

"Technically," Spinelli said, hissing and pulling his hand away, "you can't fire a fricking arrow, but some sock-sucker definitely shot one." He didn't want to tell her that it was a Girl Guide, for obvious reasons.

"Did you kill them, Jack?" Stella asked, for she knew what her husband was capable of, and it seemed like something he would do.

"I was about to," he said, "but then the wind got up a bit and blew me down the street. By the time I got back, the bastards were gone." He walked across to a mini-bar[1] and poured himself a large brandy. "I'm going to fricking find them, though, and when I do... well, you know how this usually goes."

Stella nodded. "I'm assuming some whacking will take place," she said. "Oh, Jack, I'm so pleased you didn't stop for fish-and-chips on the way home. I'm almost ecstatic that you were shot in the hand with an arrow. Is that wrong?"

Spinelli frowned, for he didn't know the right answer.

"I'm going to bed, Jack," she said, making her way back across the large living room, by which time she was exhausted and pondered whether it would be easier just to sleep on the floor where she stood. "Are you coming?"

"Yeah, in a while," he said. "I've got a few calls I need

---

[1] Well, a maxi-bar, really, on account it stored over two-hundred bottles of vintage wine and spirits, and a couple of Bud-Lights for when he was feeling particularly self-loathing.

to make, then I'll be in. Say, why don't you put that frilly thing on. You know? That frilly thing I saw laid out on the bed this morning."

"That was a doily, Jack," Stella said. "I think we inherited it from the mother that you had whacked. It's under the kettle in the kitchen now."

"Oh," Spinelli said.

"I mean, I can try to put it on, if you want me to—"

"No, it's fine," he said, picking up the phone. "You go to bed. I'll be ten minutes, tops."

No sooner had Stella left than Jack began to dial. It was difficult to do with the bandage on, since they still owned a rotary dial phone and he couldn't quite get his finger into the holes. After several attempts, he switched to his good hand and decided he should have done that to begin with.

The phone rang and rang.

And then it rang some more, by which time Spinelli could hear snoring emanating from the bedroom and rolled his eyes accordingly.

Just when he thought no one was going to answer—the fiftieth or sixtieth ring, it was—there came a sleepy voice, and it said, sleepily, "Do you have any idea what time it is?"

Spinelli didn't, because his watch had blood in it, and neither did he care, because he was Jack fricking Spinelli and if he wanted to make calls in the dead of night, he bloody well would do. "Listen to me, you nine-fingered prick," he said. "Don't make me come over there and bash your head in with the fricking phone in your hand—"

"Mr Spinelli!" came the reply. "I didn't know it was you!" He sounded flustered, and rightly so. Spinelli could hear Vinnie 'The Jockstrap' Aiello throwing himself out of bed.

"Of course you didn't know it was me, Vinnie," Spinelli said. "Now listen up."

Vinnie listened up.

"About that fricking money you owe me... yeah, the money that cost you a fricking finger... how would you like that debt to go away?"

Vinnie told him that he would very much like it to go away. In fact, he wanted it to go away more than he wanted anything to go away in the whole world.

"Meet me at the club in the morning," Spinelli said, glancing down at his watch. It was, unsurprisingly, still not function as a watch should. "Nine o'clock, or thereabouts, I don't fricking know. Oh, and Vinnie?"

"Yes, Mister Spinelli?"

"Bring me a new fricking watch."

10

There are three main bars on Mount Olympus, one of which is, for some reason, Irish-themed, and so we're not going to explain what goes on there, other than a lot of jigging, a lot of cursing, more drinking than you can shake a shillelagh at—and people have tried—and a lot of shouting and screaming at the television whenever Eurovision is on. The other two bars—The Ulysses and Duck and The Wagon and Chariot— are Greek-themed, or, since this is Greece, just regular old bars. And it is to The Ulysses and Duck where we find ourselves now, not least because it's 2-4-1 night on all cocktails and very occasionally a fight breaks out.

At the bar sat an old man, staring into space and wondering whether the 2-4-1 deal extended to Ouzo.

"That's Zeus!" one man said as he entered the bar with his wife.

"Was it the thunderbolt that gave it away?" replied his wife, "or the people running up to him with punnets of grapes? Perhaps it is the fact he is twice the size of everyone else? Come on, you buffoon. I'm going to miss the start of my dominoes match."

And it *was* Zeus, and Zeus was in a foul mood, for the whole thing with Artemis was royally pissing about with his head and he did not know how best to deal with it. He could not believe she would betray him like this, and what made it worse was that Poseidon, his own brother, had failed him, too. I mean, if you can't trust your own brother to pursue your daughter down from the heavens and onto the face of the Earth and bring her back before she got herself into all sorts of shenanigans, then who can you trust?

"Getcha another one?" asked the bartender, an affable chap known to his mates as Costas, but to Zeus he was just Barman with the Funny Eyes, for they went both ways at once. Those eyes had, as a result, seen a lot of things. Twice as much as people with regular eyes.

"Keep 'em coming," Zeus said, nudging his empty glass in Costas' general direction.

"Rough day?"

"Are you talking to me?" Zeus said, for the bartender's eyes were all over the shop. "And if so, could you please stop it."

Costas had worked at The Ulysses and Duck for almost ten years, and had grown accustomed to being told what to do by the gods. Normally, he would have obeyed Zeus without question, but today was not a normal day for Costas.

It had all started, as most days start, with a morning, and upon that very morning he had taken, as he was wont to do whenever he was feeling particularly flush, his last two drachmas down to the local corner shop and purchased a bottle of Sprite, two halloumi and onion pasties, and a scratch-card. Now, the scratch-card perhaps wasn't the best thing to spend his last two drachmas on, for now he had nothing to scratch it with, and so he took to the streets on a quest to find something with a sharp edge. The first three people he asked told him to piss off but, as luck would have it, the fourth person—who said his name was Jason something-or-other and that he was off to form a band of heroic soldiers called the Argienowts, or something—happened to be carrying a sword, and said he would be delighted to help scratch Costas' card, so long as they split any winnings fifty-

fifty.

"Sounds good to me," Costas had told the man, and so Jason had unsheathed his sword, with some proficiency Costas noted, and went to work on the bit of card.

"We've won!" Jason said, popping his sword away and examining the scratch-card as if it were a birth certificate and he had just found out his parents weren't, in fact, related.

Now Costas, who had never won a damn thing in his life[1], rejoiced. He rejoiced until his sandals fell off and he had to have a little sit down to catch his breath. By which time, Jason had cashed the scratch-card and had returned carrying two bags of drachmas.

"Now I don't have to go off in search of the golden fleece!" Jason had said, tossing Costas his share. "Didn't fancy it anyway, if I'm telling the truth, which I am." And off he went, as happy as a minotaur in shit, leaving Costas standing in the middle of the market,

---

[1] He even came second in a Costas lookalike contest, because the other bloke looked much more like Costas than Costas did.

slightly dumbfounded.

Just then, a voice had carried across the market, and since Costas' ears were far better than his eyes, inasmuch as they stayed in the right place at all times, he caught the words, "Golden fleece! Come and get your golden fleece! Lovely bit of fleece made of gold!

Costas didn't know much about golden fleeces. In fact, the first time he'd heard it used in a sentence was a moment ago, just before Jason took to his heels. But it sounded like it might be worth a few bob, and so he rushed across the market, following the vendor's proclamations and trying desperately not to tread in camel shit.

"Come and get your golden fleece!" the vendor had said as Costas slowed to a breathless halt in front of his stall.

"You're a big fella," said the vendor, lowering the golden fleece.

"Picked up three inches of camel shit on the way here," he told the vendor. "About that golden fleece—"

"Ah!" the vendor had said. "This is not for a man like you." He lifted the golden fleece again, and Costas could see that, yes, it was a fleece, and yes, it was golden. All above board, he thought. "It is for a prince, a hero, a legend."

To which Costas replied by dropping the large bag of coins down on the vendor's table, which in turn broke and collapsed to the ground in a pile of wooden splinters[1].

"You owe me for a table," the vendor had said, dropping into a crouch and untying the hessian bag filled with, "Drachmas! So many drachmas!" The vendor tied a knot in the top of the bag, stood up, and threw the golden fleece at Costas as if it were nothing more than a Puma tracksuit, and a fake one at that. "I'm off!" he said, and he was. Costas knew he was because he watched him go.

----

[1] They have really shoddy workmanship up on Mount Olympus. This particular table had been put together by a blind man. Blind men are usually very accomplished when it comes to woodwork, but this particular blind man had been dead for three years before he even considered it as a viable career path. Fortunately, he only ever got around to making two things: a flute which only plays C# and a marketplace vendor's table. The flute is still out there somewhere, pissing off Gorgons and making a general nuisance of itself.

Costas had wrapped the golden fleece around his shoulders, trying not to smell it because no matter what you do to a fleece—coat it in gold, hang it in the Tate and call it art, cut it up and sell it as candy floss—it doesn't make it something else, and this was still very much a fleece from a sheep's back, and therefore pungent as fuck.

"So, what do you think?" Costas said, shimmying this way and that so that Zeus could take the fleece in from all available angles.

"I think you should stop prancing around in that posh coat and get me a fucking Ouzo," Zeus said, for he had listened to the whole story and was none the wiser for it. In fact, during the whole thing most of the patrons had scarpered, leaving just a dominoes match and a fella in a toga smacking shit out of a fruit machine.

"One Ouzo coming up!" Costas said, brightly, and he went away to fetch it.

Zeus glanced miserably about the place. And it was while he was glancing that his $\pi\sum\prod$ rang. He knew it was his phone because he had a special ringtone[1]. He fumbled about in his robes a bit before locating the device, by which time the second verse was kicking in and Zeus didn't hold much hope in finding anyone on the other end of the line when he answered.

"Hello?" he said. And then, "Ah, Poseidon! Good to hear from you. I trust you have matters under control... what do you mean you're going for breakfast? ... I don't care how many times she has to stop for a toilet break... look, if you can't handle this I will send someone down who can... The Ulysses and Duck, if you must know... is he the one with the funny eyes?... then yes, he's on tonight... he owes you a thousand drachmas, does he?... okay, I'll tell him... all right, but just make sure you do, because if I have to come down there and take care of this myself, I'm not going to be best pleased."

"Three drachmas please, mate," Costas said, for he had returned and now stood on the other side of the bar with his palm out and his eyes dancing around in his skull as if they were trying to get away from one

---

[1]'Medusa' by Anthrax, if you must know.

another.

Zeus covered the mouthpiece momentarily, told Costas that if he didn't fuck off for a moment while he finished his call, he'd be wearing his new golden fleece up his arse, before speaking into the $\pi\sum\prod$ once again. "You still there? Okay, good. Is she with you right now?... In that case, put her on... I don't care if she's chasing a fox, put her on." In the time it took for Artemis to come to the $\pi\sum\prod$, Zeus had necked his Ouzo and ordered three more. "Artemis? Do you have any idea the problems your causing... what tunnel?"

Just then, the line went dead.

Zeus slammed the $\pi\sum\prod$ down on the bar, along with several coins.

"Ah, daughter troubles," said Costas as he worked away at a filthy glass with an even filthier rag.

"Mind your own business," said Zeus. "Oh, and Poseidon said you owe him a thousand drachmas. Something about the fruit machine not paying out last time he was in here."

Costas' jovial expression slipped from his face like an owl sliding down a well-polished window. He slipped the golden fleece from his back and thrust it across the bar at Zeus. "These things come and go, but at least I'll always have my health."

A moment later, a broken fruit machine slammed into him, killing him outright.

Zeus finished his drinks before setting off back up the mountain.

11

A room hung with pictures is a room hung with thoughts. At least, according to the famous quote. At the top of Mount Olympus, in the house of the gods, there is a room of such misery, such ghastliness, that Hera has stopped hoovering in there and now refuses to pick up all the weapons littering the floor.

Upon its walls do not hang thoughts, but there are plenty of pictures. Paintings featuring great battles of our time. At the head of a bed hangs 'The Massacre of Chios' by Eugène Delacroix, and in a triptych running along the wall are Benjamin West's 'The Death of General Wolfe', Salvador Dali's 'The Face of War', and Pablo Picasso's 'Guernica'. Not the real ones, of course, as they would have cost a fortune, but decent replicas nonetheless.

It is a room in which Ares spends much of his time plotting, causing mayhem, and generally being a bit of a git.

"Your go," Ares told Apollo, handing him the dice. "And if I catch you moving an extra space this time, I'll run you through with my sword, put your head on a stake, and set fire to the rest of you so that Zeus and Hera will have to order a dentist come take a look at the remains."

"It's just Ludo," Apollo said, rolling the dice. "Why do you have to take everything so seriously?"

Ares was too busy counting the number of spaces Apollo was taking to answer. Once Apollo had finished his turn, and content that the bastard hadn't cheated, Ares snatched up the dice and said, "Because, brother-mine, there are too many so-called gods in this family who are happy to sit around, doing nothing, allowing the humans to decide their destinies, and," —he rolled the dice— "oooh, a six!"

"Your rage will get the better of you, Ares," Apollo said, to which Ares responded by leaping to his feet and tossing the Ludo board up into the air, where it smashed against his ceiling and came back down as a jigsaw.

"Do not talk to me about rage in my own quarters," he said, furious at his brother, and in fact everything else, really.

"Take your spear away from my throat," Apollo

said.

"Oh, sorry about that," Ares replied, slowly lowering the weapon. "Force of habit, you see. Fortunately for you, I've still got the safety on." He pulled a cork from the end of the spear and tossed it out the window. A window which, had it been shut, you would have seen upon't the faint outline of a rather unfortunate owl. "Oh, I don't know why I want to fight all the time," he went on. "It's what I was created for. I am the God of War! See, it's even in the job description. Which is why it pisses me off that I'm not down there right now, stirring shit up, just like I did when I planted, then removed, then planted, then removed, then lost completely, those weapons of mass destruction in Iraq. It's in my immortal blood to cause conflict. I am an infuriated beast, caged like one of those pathetic creatures the humans stare out through bars and say "Want a nut? Want a nut?" to repeatedly, when in fact the creature does not want a nut. It wants to break free of its shackles and tear the humans apart, or at least have a go at it."

"Your spear is at my throat again," Apollo said,

calmly pushing aside the sharp bit and trying not to cut his finger in the process.

"See!" Ares said, once again lowering the spear. "It's a wonder I haven't taken your eye out with this thing. All I want is a good war, you know? A real battle, like we did in the old days. On horseback, with catapults and fire and people ducking so they didn't get hit by the fiery things catapulting at them."

"It is a time machine you want, brother," Apollo said, climbing to his feet. "And I fear those good old days of which you speak are well and truly behind us. The humans have done nothing to warrant an apocalypse—"

"But it would do them the world of good," Ares said. "There are far too many of them anyway, and most of them are bastards—"

"It is that kind of blanket definition which does not go down well with Father," Apollo said, making for the door before he lost an eye. "Control your rage, brother-mine. Find a new hobby. I've heard there is a golden fleece out there somewhere. Gather an army of heroes and go find it. Go on a little boat-trip. I'm sure it's not far, and your adventure will most likely not result in the deaths of thousands. In fact, I should imagine that most of your adversaries will already be of the dead variety. Smash some skeletons up. Go on, enjoy yourself!"

Ares shook his head, for he was not cut out for heroics. "I fear I am destined to stir shit up," he said. "And that, no matter how hard I try, nothing will sate me quite like it."

Apollo was now half out the door; his own quarters were just across the hallway. It would be far easier finding them if he had two functioning eyes with which to work. "Then I fear you are a lost cause," he said, and with that he quickly yanked the door shut and legged it just as something long and hard and pointy at one end thumped into it.

12

The day started, as it so often does, with a morning, and upon that morning, Simian Knight lay unconscious on his sofa, his chin encrusted with drool and his face red and folded over in several places, the way it so often is when you've slept upon anything less comfortable than a bed. He groaned, almost choked on his own tongue, groaned again, had a lovely but brief little dream about a piece of bread which, when dropped, always landed butter side up, and then groaned a third time, more for dramatic effect than anything.

Outside, beyond his Venetian blinds and mainly monochrome existence, the world was waking up. Well, not the *whole* world, as it was still night-time in much of it, but the half facing the sun was rising, and the half still in the dark didn't envy it one bit.

Birdsong could be heard, and off in the distance so could sirens, for this was London, and not some Disney fairy-tale. The hobos weren't all about to break into autotuned arias about how wonderful it was to be alive—although if they did, they might have found their lives exponentially enriched—and there was no beating of dusty mats from windows high above the city, because the mayor had outlawed that nonsense years ago.

Simian groaned again, unaware of the city waking all around him.

Up in the sky, the clouds parted momentarily to allow those early risers a glimpse of the sun, before snatching it away again a moment later, and saying, "That's enough for today. Now we're going to piss on you for several hours. You're very welcome."

In other words, it was a normal day in the city. Tourists came from all four corners of the planet to watch the hobos not sing, to witness the momentary parting of the clouds and then the hours of intermittent rain. They liked nothing more than to watch the natives fight over parking spaces, of which there were so few that people had taken to parking at home and catching the bus to work. Tourists, those rubbernecking bastards. London could not get enough of them.

Halfway across the city, the Queen was rousing to

the sound of Phillip grunting incoherently as he scraped the last dregs of Winalot into the corgis' bowls. In a moment she would pop off to the royal throne for her morning shit, but for now she just stared at the window, wondering how the other half lived and deciding it probably wasn't for her and that she was probably better off spending her time concentrating on not dying.

Simian Knight snorted twice, drooled a bit, said, "Biscuits!" for no apparent reason, then went back to snoring fitfully.

In an alleyway not too far away, a fox with its mouth fused shut watched as a hobo crawled reluctantly from beneath the newspapers he called a bed, got to his feet, and proceeded to stretch and yawn noisily before breaking into song. It didn't last long, for a shoe whipped suddenly across the alley and caught the hobo a good one to the temple. He went down like a sack of potatoes, and would spend the rest of the day regretting his decision to wail out Whitney Houston's 'I Have Nothing' at the top of his tar-infused lungs.

Simian's eyes flew open and he bolted upright,

staring around the office and wondering how he came to be there and how much capital he would need in order to create a piece of bread which always landed butter-side up, no matter how hard you threw it at the carpet.

"Wha... whe... ho..." For some strange reason, he could not finish his questions. He quickly discovered this was because of all the gunk around his mouth and headed for the bathroom to wash his face. Once he had washed his face, he glanced upon his reflection in the mirror and said, "What? Where? How?" and once he had that out of his system, he stared into his own eyes[1] for a few moments, trying to retrace his steps from the previous night.

It was all very fuzzy at first, with lots of blurred images and more than one which appeared to have been created in Microsoft Paint. He could not for the life of him recall anything about last night.

"Toilet!" he said. Fortunately the toilet didn't

---

[1] There had once been a man on Mount Olympus who could do this, but he had been unceremoniously squashed by a broken fruit-machine, and the rest, as they say, is history.

answer back, because Simian wasn't hoping for a conversation; he was merely naming the thing upon which he sat when he liked to contemplate, to ponder things ever-so-slightly beyond his grasp, and sometimes to play Angry Birds. The toilet was his second desk. He liked it quite a bit, not least because it was far less cluttered than his first desk. Also, his first desk didn't have a flusher.

He took down his trousers and penguin-walked across to the toilet. A smart man would have done this in reverse order, but Simian liked to live dangerously. Sitting down, he sighed with relief, and then found himself wondering what the Queen was doing at that exact moment, in her beautiful palace just a few miles away. If he had known that she too was on the toilet—straining and moaning, one foot up on the sink and the other balanced precariously upon a corgi—it might have changed his opinion of her somewhat, but he did not and could not know, which was probably for the best.

"Think, think, think..." And he thought, thought, thought, but he could not remember anything until...

something about a millipede... a millipede that went, 'Rargh!" Deciding he was muddying the waters even more, he went back to basics. It was while he was going back to basics that the phone upon his desk began to ring. "Damn!" he said, and, "Blast!" because this always happened when he was contemplating at his second desk. Ironically, it never happened while he was sat at his first desk, where the telephone lived. He made a mental note to have a second phone installed—it wouldn't look great, right there next to the toilet-roll-holder, but Simian valued convenience over aesthetics any day of the week[1]—before launching himself to his feet and penguin-walking his way out of the bathroom and across to his desk, where he proceeded to pull his trousers up before picking up the phone.

"Goodbye?" he said, which wasn't right at all, so he gave it another go. "Hello?"

"It's me," whispered a voice, and left it at that.

"Good for you!" Simian said, for if there was one

---

[1] Which is why there is a toaster next to the bathtub, a toothbrush in the cutlery drawer, and one of those 'OPEN-CLOSED' signs hanging upon his office door, but on this one both sides said CLOSED.

thing he admired more than anything it was self-awareness.

"Did you get it?" the voice whispered.

There passed between them a moment of awkward silence, during which time Simian managed to tidy the papers strewn across his desk and make a rather long chain out of black-and-white paperclips. "Erm," he said. "Who did you say was calling again?"

"It's me!" the voice angrily whispered.

"Yes, yes, I know that," Simian said, annoyedly. "But, well, you see, something strange happened last night and I'm only just starting to pick up the pieces. To be quite honest with you, it took me a while to recall who, in fact, *I* was upon waking." Perhaps it would have been time better spent, he thought, if I had figured that out before I started wondering what the Queen was up to.

"It's Stella," whispered the voice.

"Stella, Stella, Stella—"

"Spinelli!"

"Ah, yes!" Simian said, and then, "Oh!"

Fragments of the previous night began to form in his mind. The whole thing sent a chill down his spine.

"Well?" said Stella. "Did you get it? When Jack came back last night I could smell batter on him. He was with her, and since I've paid you a handsome sum up front, which stands a rather good chance of not bouncing when you cash it, I assume you managed to capture their little rendezvous on film?"

"Yes," Simian said, "I mean, no, not exactly." Then it all came flooding back in the most cliched of ways. Simian dropped the phone, yanked his coat off and then his shirt, before proceeding to finger the open wound in his shoulder and cry out like a hungry child as he did so.

Only there *was* no open wound, and after several seconds of watching his life flash before his eyes for the second time in as many days, he picked up the phone and said, "Stella! Something very strange is going on! I think... I think I am going mad!"

"Shh!" Stella said. "Jack's in the bathroom. He might hear you."

Simian didn't care if Jack Spinelli heard him. In fact, he said, "Ask your husband if he knows of any good psychologists!" for he had seen The Sopranos, and it was therefore a well-known fact that mafia bosses and London gangsters alike often turned to shrinks when they reached breaking point.

"What do you mean you're going mad?" Stella asked.

"Last night!" Simian said. "I remember it all now so very vividly. I was hiding in a bush..."

"Yes?"

"And I was waiting for Spinelli to turn up to meet the hot red-headed in front the chip-shop."

"Go on."

"And there was this millipede which jumped out of the bush and went 'Rargh!', and I said to it—"

"Skip the millipede part," Stella whispered.

"Okay," Simian said, pouring himself a large whiskey and lighting a cigarette, and feeling immediately better for it. "Okay, well, here goes," he said, knocking his first shot back and refilling his glass, "Spinelli arrived, and I knew I had him bang to rights, so I just started snapping, you know? Just snapping away, I think if you put all the pictures together and flick through them really quickly, it'd be like watching a re-enactment of what I'm telling you right now."

"So you did get the pictures," Stella said, barely able to contain her excitement.

"Yes, yes, but forget about all that," Simian said, pausing only to take a long draw on his cigarette. "I was in the bush taking pictures when, out of nowhere and completely unwarranted, might I add, I took to my shoulder what can only be described as an arrow. I know how crazy this sounds, but—"

"An arrow," Stella said, though it was not quite a question. It was more conversational than that. Kind of like, "Oh, an arrow. Yes, we're all taking arrows to our bodies at the moment. You are in fact no one until you've taken an arrow, mwah, mwah, mwah."

"Yes," Simian said. "An arrow."

"Jack was at the hospital much of last night," Stella said. She was no longer whispering, though her voice was low enough to fall under the banner of surreptitious. "Said 'some frickin' sock-sucker shot me with an arrow', or something like that. I can't do impressions, sorry."

"No, that was really good," Simian said, although it

wasn't. "So Spinelli got shot too, huh?" Something about this made him very happy. Perhaps it was knowing that the person holding the bow was indiscriminate, and that there wasn't, in fact, already a contract out on him. "But this all gets weirder, I'm afraid," he said, placing himself firmly back on topic. "I think... I'm almost certain that I saw the person who shot me."

"What did he look like?" Stella said. "Jack'll bloody murder him."

"It was a Girl Guide," Simian said, "accompanied by a big guy wearing a white robe and with a long, white beard. That one was carrying a bloody great big fork. And a woman bathed all in gold who appeared to be rather good at stitch-work." He glanced down at the spot where, last night, there had been an arrow, saw no scab, no gash, no stitches, and in fact not a mark, before adding, "Although I might have dreamt the whole thing."

There was a momentary silence, in which Simian could just about make out the discordant warbling of a man singing in the shower, and then Stella said, with some incredulity, "A Girl Guide?"

"Yes."

"And an old man in a white robe with a long white beard carrying a big fork?"

"Yes, I can see," said Simian, "why you're having trouble believing me. It does sound rather ridiculous put like that."

"Might I suggest laying off the booze before 8 a.m.?" she said.

"My dear Mrs Spinelli," Simian said with a little laugh. "I am a private investigator, a PI, a dick, a gumshoe."

"You're certainly *one* of those things," she said, to which Simian did not have a witty retort.

"It is in my blood to partake in hard liquor at unsociable hours and smoke sixty cigarettes a day. What, if not whiskey, would you have me drink?"

"I hear Tizer's a suitable replacement," she said. "But we are getting off track here, Mr Knight. When would it be possible for me to collect the photographs?"

Simian had to hand it to the dame; she knew what

she wanted, and right now she wanted proof her husband's infidelity so that she could drag him through the divorce courts quicker than you can say Harry Ramsden, and therefore lay claim to half his assets, amounting to roughly most of London, a bit of Kent, and a delightful smallholding on the Wabash, wherever the hell that was.

Simian glanced down at the camera sitting upon his desk and thought, *My second desk doesn't have a camera*. Then he said, "How does this afternoon sound?"

"It sounds very good indeed, Mr Knight," she said. "Now, I must go. Jack is out of the shower and will want his bandage changing. Until this afternoon... adieu."

"I'm very sorry, Mrs Spinelli," Simian said. "I do not speak Somali. However, I will bid you macsalaamo[1] until this afternoon." He waited a moment before adding, "No, *you* hang up... no you... *you* hang up..." and, after realising that he was talking to himself, he hung up.

He sat back in his chair, sighed, and thought, for a

---

[1] In fact, he does speak Somali, and therein lies the gag.

moment, that he wasn't going completely mad after all. There was a perfectly reasonable explanation for everything that had happened the night before, he was sure of it. "A bit of undigested cheese," he said, in his best Ebenezer Scrooge voice. Impressions were not his forte, either.

He stood, and was about to return to the bathroom when he saw, upon the carpet, a perfectly round, golden burn roughly the diameter of a serving platter. He said, "Oh," and then, "a gilt crop-circle," neither of which made him feel better about it, and so he decided to have a little lie down instead, right there where he stood.

In other words he passed out, fainted away, keeled over, and hoped the people in the office below didn't mind all the noise as he went.

*

In the office below fifty geriatrics wandered aimlessly around, occasionally bumping into one another and even more occasionally apologising for it. Each of them held in their arthritic hand a ticket, upon which was printed a number.

"If you'd all like to take a seat," said the receptionist, a woman whose tan was so extreme she looked like the Stay Puft Marshmallow man after a rather violent campfire.

"There aren't any seats," replied one elderly gent.

"I think she wants us to sit on the floor," said another.

"If you would," said the receptionist, "that would be great."

"I'm not sitting on the floor!" one old lady said. "If I get down there, I'm never getting back up again."

They went back and forth like this for almost five minutes until the receptionist, by way of an irate sigh, went off to fetch some chairs.

DODGE & E. PACEMAKERS LTD. had been in business for a little over a year and, in that time, they had lost most of their customers. The company's CEO, Bartleby Dodge, put the loss down to the fact that the company dealt primarily with old people, and had nothing, no, *absolutely* nothing to do with the company's bestselling device running on two AA batteries and a soupcon of willpower. "Part of the reason why our pacemakers are so cheap," his sales spiel went, "is that it works on collaboration with the person whose body it finds itself in. You must *want* to live, and the pacemaker will continue to function correctly. Start looking at over-60's life insurance and pottering about in the garden, the device picks up on it and starts to reduce in functionality." In other words, so long as you don't think of death, the device will be just fine.

Which, at the concept stage, seemed like a fantastic idea. But it was at the concept stage where the whole thing collapsed, since old people like to think of death on a daily basis. They just can't help themselves. Every new book they start might go unfinished, every time they go to bed they wonder whether they'll wake up the next morning, every time one of their friends die they said things like, "I can't believe it. He was only ninety!" and, "You never know when it's your turn."

Yes, old people almost *fantasise* about death, and so the DPMU[1] units, the company's top seller, tended to stop trying after only a few hours, on account of the

---

[1] Dodge PaceMaker Ultimate, although the only ultimate thing about it is the cost.

donor not meeting them halfway.

"How long have we been waiting?" asked an old lady who was bent over like a question mark.

"Almost five minutes," said an old man who was trying to hammer a packet of humbugs out of an ATM. "This thing's not working," he said. "It's swallowed fifteen guineas and a sixpence so far."

Just then, there came an almighty thud on the ceiling above, and fifty hands—some clenching tickets with numbers printed on them—went to fifty chests in unison. It was like watching some strange geriatric version of the Thriller video. One of them even went, "Huh!" You had to be there, really.

When the receptionist returned a moment later with a stack of chairs and still cursing under her breath for having to go out and fetch them, she saw, upon the floor, fifty dead old people, which only made her curse even more-so, for now she had to take the chairs back.

Over a speaker somewhere in the room, a man's voice said, "Ticket number one, please."

13

A few streets away, in a much nicer office, Spinelli sat behind his desk running wads of money through one of those machines that goes, "Drrrrrrrrrrr-ta-da!" as it counts. Opposite him, standing either side of the door, stood his nameless associates. They had names, he just didn't know what they were, and it wasn't important. What was important was that they didn't interrupt him when he was running wads of money through the machine that went, "Drrrrrrrrrrr-ta-da!" because it fairly put him in a bad mood.

"What time is it," Spinelli asked without looking up.

One of the men said, "Five-to-nine, Mr Spinelli," but, for the life of him, Spinelli didn't know which, for they had almost identical speaking voices. There was perhaps a quarter of an octave in it, but who can discern between a quarter of an octave, really?[1]

Spinelli was about to put out a contract on Vinnie 'The Jockstrap' Aiello for failing to arrive five minutes

---

[1] Other than the Greater Wax Moth, but who's going to trust the word of a creature whose entire diet consists of plastic carrier bags?

before he was due, when there came upon the door a rather tentative knock. It was the knock of a man who didn't want to be there, the rapping of a man whose life was probably flashing before his eyes right now, and the knock of a man who was presently shitting bricks. The knock was followed by a hesitant squeak, and Spinelli said to his men, "Let him in."

As Vinnie walked into the office, he had about him a pallid look, a sick look, the look of a man who was already clocking the exits and deciding that there was only one, and he'd just walked voluntarily through it. Of course, it had been entrance back then, but now it was an exit, and there were two big bastards blocking it.

Spinelli looked up for the first time in ten minutes and smiled. The machine sitting in front of him went, "Drrrrrrrrrr-ta-da!" one last time before falling silent. "What's the matter, Vinnie?" he said. "You look as if you've seen a ghost."

"I... I brought you a watch, Mr Spinelli," Vinnie said, and with that he produced the watch from his pocket, placed it upon the desk, and gave it a little nudge in

Spinelli's general direction.

Spinelli looked down at it and sighed. "Is that Mickey Mouse?" he said.

"I believe it is, Mr Spinelli, yes," said Vinnie. "His arms are the hour and minute hands," he added, as if that might help to sell the watch.

"I can see that, Vinnie," Spinelli said. "What I can't see, however, is the gigantic pair of fricking balls sitting on my desk, which is what it must have taken for you to bring this fricking watch to me and expect me to wear it."

Vinnie visibly tightened and took his hands off the desk. He had nine fingers remaining and wanted to keep it that way. "It's a very expensive watch, Mr Spinelli," Vinnie said, and then, "Vintage."

Spinelli looked at the watch, which appeared to be keeping good time, and then at Vinnie, who appeared to be sweating profusely and mouthing the Lord's Prayer. Then he removed his broken Rolex and threw it across the room. One of his men caught it—the one who always stood on the left—and secreted it in his suit pocket. The one on the right looked enviously across to his colleague before remembering he was still winning in the Mom department. He could therefore keep the watch.

"I quite like it," Spinelli said, attaching the Mickey Mouse watch to his wrist. "It *says* something about me."

"That you're mean, but you have a playful side?" Vinnie ventured, relaxing slightly and dabbing at his brow with a hankie.

"If I wanted people to think I have a playful side," Spinelli said, "I'd cut their fingers off and replace them with Pez dispensers." He thought about that for a moment, wondered if there was a market for such things, then wrote it off as a bad bet. "No, this watch says, 'Fuck with me and I'll bend your fricking arms around until you're reading a quarter to thirteen.'"

"Yes," Vinnie said, "I suppose it does say that."

"Now," said Spinelli, leaning in, his face framed by all the cash precariously balanced on the desk. "That proposition I told you about last night still stands."

Vinnie nodded, and he looked, Spinelli thought, a little like one of those things arseholes put on their car's dashboard.

"I will write off your fricking debt, Vinnie," he said, "if you find the sock-suckers who did this to me and make them disappear." He held his bandaged hand aloft, and Vinnie gazed upon it, seemingly mesmerised.

"Who am I looking for?" Vinnie asked. "Was it Paulie Pagoda? Johnny "Three Tits" Maroni?" And he continued to reel off the entire cast of London Mobsters as Spinelli wondered how he was going to tell Vinnie that it wasn't rival families, it wasn't disgruntled dealers, it wasn't gangbangers or thugs, but the work of a twelve-year-old girl in a Guides uniform and what he presumed to be her grandfather. He thought about it, but there was no easy way of saying it, and so, as Vinnie moved onto the cast of *The Sopranos*, Spinelli interrupted him with:

"A little girl!" He leaned back in his chair, which squeaked beneath his weight. "It was a little fricking girl and an old fricking man."

For a few seconds, Vinnie just sat there. He sat there and he frowned, and he rolled a few words around his mouth before not speaking, and then he scratched at his head with a finger that wasn't there anymore, and finally he said, "A little girl and an old man?"

"Did I fricking stutter?" Spinelli said, for he was fairly embarrassed by it all and yet knew he had to maintain his gangster bravado. "But they weren't working alone," he went on. "Some asshole was trying to take pictures of me from a bush," he said, "and I was about to whack him when his friends intervened. That's how I got this—" he held his bandaged hand aloft once more "—and that's why I want you track down these fricking sock-suckers and make them pay."

"You want me to bury them with the fishes?" Vinnie asked.

"No, the pet cemetery is full," Spinelli said, which tugged at his heartstrings a little. "You remember Flopsy?"

Vinnie nodded, but he had a look about him, Spinelli noticed, which suggested he wouldn't know Flopsy if you put him in a line-up of two.

"No, I want you to find them, chop them up, put

them in suitcases and throw them in the fricking Thames," Spinelli said, lighting a fat cigar, but only after making a show of snipping its end off. "But I have to warn you, Vinnie. This isn't just a little girl and an old man I'm talking about. I think the old guy can control wind."

"Good for him," Vinnie said. "Most of them can't."

"The girl, she shot me with a fricking arrow from a hundred yards away," Spinelli said, chewing at his cigar.

"I blame the schools," Vinnie said. "And *The Hunger Games*."

"Do you think you can manage this, Vinnie?"

"I don't," Vinnie said, "anticipate it being a problem." He lit a cigarette and exhaled a plume of smoke into the room. "But if I do this," he said, "the debt is gone forever. No takeses backses."

"You have my word," Spinelli said, which they both knew wasn't worth the paper it wasn't printed it.

"Then we have a deal, M Spinelli," Vinnie said, reaching across the desk and shaking Spinelli's bandage with his own recently-disfigured hand. They both hissed a little, then remembered where they were and tried to forget the whole embarrassing episode.

"Can one of you boys," Spinelli said, "show Vinnie to the door."

The boys couldn't decide which one of them was going to do it, so they both did.

"Oh, and Vinnie?" Spinelli said.

Vinnie turned around and said, "Yes, Mr Spinelli?"

"You have twenty-four hours," he said, winding up his new Mickey Mouse watch. "If those sock-suckers ain't dead by this time tomorrow, it'll be *you* in the fricking Thames. Capeesh?"

Vinnie said that he didn't speak French, but that he had the gist of it and that there was absolutely nothing to worry about, the job was as good as done.

Spinelli, now alone in his office, began running wads of notes through the machine that went, "Drrrrrrrrrr-ta-da!" again, occasionally glancing down at his new watch and smiling.

"Playful," he said. "Very fricking playful."

*

Once outside, Vinnie sucked in great big lungfuls of air,

which was a terrible idea as London air is just a few Sieverts short of that still floating about Chernobyl. He quickly spluttered, doubled over, and upchucked onto the back of a fox who had been hiding, apparently, behind the bins at the back of SPINELLI'S. The fox didn't seem to care. In fact, it was one of them most lugubrious foxes Vinnie had ever seen. It simply stared at the sick dripping from its back, down its side, and onto the ground next to it, and shrugged, which was a shame as Vinnie felt really bad about it.

A little girl, an old man, and a pervert hiding in the bushes in London? How hard could it be?

Vinnie walked along the passageway and out onto the main street in front of the bar. Everywhere he looked there were little girls, and where there *wasn't* one there stood an old man instead. Quite what had happened to all the middle-aged people was beyond Vinnie, and he would have to really get stuck in if he wanted to rustle every bush in the city, thusly causing any hider within to leap out and perhaps go, "Argh!"

"This is bollocks," he huffed, walking through the crowd. Little girl, old man, little girl, old man, little girl, old man. He felt like Scooby Doo running along a corridor, the background on repeat to save money and workflow for the animators.

"I'm as good as dead," he said.

His phone began to ring.

*

"Hey, Vinnie?" Spinelli said, phone pressed to his ear. "I forgot to mention something. The girl might be wearing a Girl Guides uniform and the old guy might be wearing a long flowing white robe and sandals... yeah, fricking sandals... I know, right! Anyway, just thought I'd let you know... okay, fuck off!"

*

Vinnie brightened. That narrowed it down a bit. On through the crowd he went, practically skipping now, and whistling, and feeling generally upbeat. He said, "Tits!" and, "Buggeration!" a moment later when he saw, as luck wouldn't have it, a troop of Guides making their way across the street in one direction and, behind them, a long line of old men stepping down from a parked-up coach, upon whose side was printed

JESUS LOOKALIKE WORLD TOUR 2017[1].

"Typical," Vinnie said, glancing down at his nine remaining fingers for what might have been the very last time.

---

[1] Not much of a World Tour, as it started in Hackney and terminated in Stepney, stopping at a pub halfway for a jar of jellied eels and a pint of piss-warm beer.

14

The full-English breakfast is sold in over one million establishments across the country, from city-centre high-streets to laybys on the M25. Like rats, you are never more than six feet away from a heart-attack inducing morning meal, which is probably why the rats are there in the first place, eagerly waiting for the moment you drop a chunk of black-pudding.

Artemis and Poseidon sat in such an establishment, watching the humans as they set about their breakfasts like zoo animals. All around, people nattered and mumbled and poured mountains of salt onto their bacon, while a radio behind the counter blasted out Coldplay's latest suicidal ballad, just in case the patrons were feeling extra chirpy and needed taking down a peg or two.

"This place is awful," Poseidon said, browsing a ketchup-coated menu. "I can't believe they have the audacity to call this stuff food."

Artemis, on the other hand, was having a field-day. She watched as one man forced three sausages into his mouth whole before masticating[1]. "Are you kidding me?" she said, throwing a handful of salt across her shoulder, for no other reason than she 'd just watched a builder do it, and it seemed like fun. "This place is fantastic. For the first time ever I feel alive."

"Order something from this menu," Poseidon said, "and that feeling will quickly disappear."

Just then, and as if by some sort of magical illusion, a short, stout lady with a cigarette jutting from her mouth and a tattoo on her forearm featuring a Lovecraftian deity[2], appeared and said, in a voice that was neither male nor female but a combination of the two, "Couple of full-Englishes, is it?" She tapped a half-chewed pencil impatiently upon the notepad in her hand, and it was at this point Artemis noticed she was missing a thumb.

"Can we have five more minutes," Poseidon said. "Is there... is there a wine list we could peruse?"

The waitress glanced down at Poseidon with furrowed eyebrows. "I'll bring it right over," she said,

---

[1] In public, no less!
[2] She was the girl with the Dagon tattoo.

and Poseidon's face lit up, but then she said, "would you like any caviar while you peruse the wine list? Perhaps a tray of Ferrero Rocher, neatly stacked up into a pyramid?" and Poseidon's face drooped again.

Artemis applauded excitedly. "Oh, I do love a bit of sarcasm in the mornings," she said, to which the waitress replied:

"Five more minutes. If you haven't ordered a full-English by then, you're out on your ear. I've got builders and street-walkers to feed, for crying out loud." And with that she turned, tucked the half-chewed pencil behind a half-chewed ear, and bounded across the room to rearrange the *Daily Sport* rack.

"That's it!" Poseidon said, wrapping a hand around his trident, which had been leaning against an old man's mobility scooter. "We're not staying here another minute. I can almost feel the fleas in my beard. I have spent the last twenty minutes watching a council-worker dig about up his nose as if intent on reaching his brain."

"I know," said Artemis. "Isn't it wonderful!"

"It most certainly is not," Poseidon said. "Is this

why you came to Earth? To be around this... this menagerie?"

Artemis nodded. "There's a full-Irish breakfast bar at the end of the street. We could finish up here and take a little walk down—"

"Have you made up your minds yet?" The waitress had returned, only now she held in her hand a dog lead, and at the end of that lead was a slobbering giant of a bear, sort of a cross between a Rottweiler and a thing that eats Rottweilers. It huffed once, snuffled up a piece of sausage someone on the adjacent table had dropped, and slumped to the ground in what could only be described as out-and-out despair.

"I would like the breakfast you have to take a toilet break halfway through," Artemis said, "and one of those black sludge things everyone seems to be drinking."

The waitress scribbled down on her notepad. "One belly-buster and a regular coffee," she said, before turning to Poseidon, who was gripping onto his trident as if it might save him from the waitress. "We've got cutlery here," she said. "Costs extra to use your own."

Poseidon released the trident, cast his gaze over the menu for the umpteenth time and, for the umpteenth time, decided he rather liked being immortal. "I'm fine, thanks," he said, pushing the menu away.

"If you're not eating," said the waitress, "then I'll have to ask you to wait outside."

Poseidon looked out through the large window to his right, saw that it was now pissing it down, and said, "Oh, fine, I'll have a pot of tea and a piece of toast." Although he doubted, when delivered to him, it would look anything like it sounded.

"That's the spirit!" Artemis said, before looking up at the waitress and adding, "If you don't mind me asking, how did you come to lose your thumb?"

The waitress frowned, and she was getting rather good at it. "What?" she said, and then, "what thumb?"

"Exactly," Artemis said. "How did you lose it?"

Looking down at her thumb, the waitress said, "Bloody hell!" before turning and rushing for the kitchen, dragging her pet bear with her, although not before it had suctioned itself to the tiles so that it could hoover up everything in its path as they went.

"See?" Artemis said to Poseidon. "Who says Earth is boring? That entire thumb episode was a lark. Nothing like that ever happens up on Olympus. You're lucky if someone has a little fall. People rejoice when a villager comes a-barrelling down the mountain[1]. Down here, things such as this happen on a daily basis. You can't move for idiots. In fact, you're never more than six feet away from one."

"I can attest to that," Poseidon said. "And I thought that was rats? You're never more than six feet away from a rat?"

"Where did you hear something as preposterous as that?" Artemis said. "How very absurd, Poseidon. Look around. Do you see, anywhere in this establishment, a rat?"

"I'll bet that's what the bear's for," he replied.

All at once someone screamed. Artemis turned just in time to see a man launch a severed thumb across the

---

[1] They also rejoice when they discover the golden fleece on a market stall and when they very occasionally come up trumps on a scratch-card, but those things almost never happen so it's not worth mentioning.

room. Her instincts suddenly took over, and a second later a thumb was pinned to the specials board by an arrow. A raucous cheer erupted about the place; Artemis blushed a little before slinging her bow and retaking her seat.

Poseidon seemed awfully embarrassed. Artemis knew he was awfully embarrassed because there was a ketchup-coated menu where his face used to be.

"One belly-buster," said the waitress, returning from the kitchen. "One piece of toast, a coffee and a pot of tea." She placed the tray down on the table, which was when Artemis noticed the stainless-steel spatula protruding from the stump where a thumb had once been. "Pay at the till on your way out, and if you try making a run for it before settling up, Grizzly loves a good chase. You'd be doing me a favour. Ain't had a chance to walk him yet this morning."

Once she had gone, Poseidon looked down at the huge oval plate in front of Artemis and said, "You're never going to eat all of that."

"Thousand drachmas says I do."

Poseidon quickly checked his bank balance, saw

that it was empty, and said, "Okay, you're on."

Three toilet breaks later, Artemis mopped up bean juice with a piece of hard bread, leaned back in her chair, and went, "Ah."

Seemingly traumatised, Poseidon said, "I have seen many things in my life. I battered Odysseus with storms after he blinded my cyclops son. I fought against the Trojans. I have watched as sailors drowned horses as a sacrifice to me, which I wasn't best pleased about as I love horses, can't get enough of them. I have battled lecherous satyrs and sat through *Percy Jackson and the Olympians*, just in case there was anything in there for which I could sue for libel. I have done all of those things, and nothing has repulsed me more than watching you scoop up a fried tomato between two pieces of stale bread and push it into your little face."

Artemis wiped grease from her chin and burped loudly, so loudly that a picture of the head chef—with the words 'In Memoriam: Big Joe, who ate here every day, at least until he keeled over dead and cost us ten-grand in refurbishment work (1980-1999)— fell from the wall and smashed into pieces. Another cheer went up around the room.

"The thing is," Artemis said, in that way she so often did when she was about to explain what the thing was, "you're repulsed by the humans and their way of life because, secretly, you envy them."

Poseidon waved her ridiculous remark away with a hand. "Nonsense," he said.

"It's true! You're secretly jealous because they don't have to conform. Take, for instance, the non-gods up on Olympus. They're happier than we are, because all they have to do is mill around all day, occasionally popping grapes into our mouths. It is such a simple existence. No one expects them to do anything else, and they're happier for it."

"Bollocks," Poseidon said, for nonsense simply didn't cut it anymore.

"Look around," Artemis said, and Poseidon, though he was loath to do so, looked around. "They're completely aloof, going about their business and not worrying about whether they're going to return home at the end of the day to find their house burned to the ground because Hephaestus got a little bit worked up and forgot to check on the furnace. They don't have to concern themselves with Krakens when they throw themselves in the sea. The most they can expect is a jellyfish sting, and now they've realised that if they piss on it the pain goes away, even that doesn't bother them. Have you ever tried pissing on a Kraken sting? I guarantee it does nothing to alleviate the pain, and not only that but you'll look stupid doing it."

"Humans don't have to worry about arriving at work, only to find everyone cowering behind the water-cooler because, 'There's a Gorgon in the conference room, and it's angry as fuck'. Their horses are horses through-and-through, not horses with human heads or horse heads on human bodies. Simplicity. In fact, it's very rare for a creature on Earth to have more than one head, so rare that when they discover one, they take pictures of it and send them in to freak-show publications for the whole world to marvel at. On the extremely odd occasion a human is born with more appendages than its parents had expected, it is packed off to join the circus, and even then it gets lodgings and a minimum wage."

"Is there a point to any of this?" Poseidon said, grabbing his trident just before the old man on his mobility scooter headed for the counter to settle his bill.

"The point is," Artemis said, "that life would be so much simpler if we were human."

"You would hand back your immortality to Zeus just because you want to piss on yourself at the seaside?"

Artemis shrugged. "Immortality has a nice ring to it, but after a certain point it does get rather tedious. Where is the peril?"

"I believe you just ate it," Poseidon said. "You're talking bollocks, Artemis, and if Zeus could hear you now he would tell you exactly what I'm about to tell you."

"And that is?"

"Never take money from family."

Artemis frowned, for she hadn't a clue what he was talking about. Poseidon knew, however, and was already planting seeds so that he might avoid paying her the thousand drachmas he didn't have in his account.

"Was everything okay?" asked the waitress as she came to clear the table, although her tone suggested she didn't really give a damn, it was more of an automatic question, ingrained in her as a result of clearing tables of empty plates for so many years.

"Beautiful!" Artemis said, patting her belly. "Had to take three toilet breaks." But the waitress was already gone, off to the kitchen to drop the plates in the industrial-sized sink from a very great height, hoping they would break so that she didn't have to wash them and could just throw them in the bin instead.

"Wonder how the gumshoe is doing this morning?" Artemis said as she mechanically dusted grains of salt from the table.

"Why do you even *care*?" Poseidon grunted. "Ten minutes from now, we'll be back on Olympus. You should be more concerned about how your father is doing, not some two-bit private-investigator you put an arrow through." After a moment, he calmly said, "I am sure he is doing fine. Aceso worked her magic, did she not?"

"Yes, but I still feel a little bad for shooting him," she said. "And then for leaving him. And also for doing nothing to fix that bloody great big burn-mark in his carpet before we left."

"That was unfortunate," Poseidon said. "I shall have to bear that in mind when calling upon Aceso in future."

"Did you know—"

"I had no idea she was going to singe the man's floor," Poseidon said. "But, as you said, humans have very little to worry about, and therefore the gumshoe is probably out there right now, standing in a carpet shop and trying to choose between eggshell blue and Arabian red."

Artemis sighed, for she had always wanted to visit a carpet shop. After a few moments of quiet contemplation, she said, "Come on then, Uncle. Settle the bill and we can go."

Poseidon's eyes widened. "I don't have any money," he said, for he didn't, not even in his Omega Bank account[1]. There is not much use for hard cash when you are a Greek God, although it does come in handy when you want to remain incognito, say when you're ordering something unsavoury from the adult section of Sky. The only other time it comes in handy is when you're making wagers with other Greek gods.

"That's okay," Artemis said. "Take it out of the two-thousand drachmas you owe me."

"Ah," said Poseidon.

"You don't have it, do you?" Artemis said. "I can't believe your making wagers with money you don't even have."

"I'm owed it," Poseidon said. "By a wonky-eyed barman, so I will definitely get it for you. I just don't have access to it right now, here, for this meal, in this place, presently."

"Ah," said Artemis, glancing across to where Grizzly sat beside the counter, licking his lips and eyeing them with some suspicion. "Well isn't this a pickle."

---

[1] In fact, a direct debit, to SKY for a PPV chariot race he had watched the previous Saturday night, had left him overdrawn by fifty drachmas.

"I could always summon a storm," Poseidon said.

"They wouldn't notice the difference," Artemis said, motioning to the window and, more specifically, the downpour on the other side of it. "No, we have no choice but to make a run for it." Her stomach didn't like the sound of that and groaned its disapproval. Yet another cheer went up around the café, and Artemis tried not to let it go to her head. "On the count of three," she said, "we'll slowly get to our feet and make our way toward the door."

Across the room, Grizzly went, "Grrrrrr," and Artemis suddenly realised the importance of only speaking out of the corner of your mouth when you didn't want anyone else to know what you were plotting.

"Nice and easy," she said, but there was nothing nice, or particularly easy, about what they were trying to do. "On three." She locked eyes with Poseidon, her backside now half-on, half-off her chair. "One..."

Poseidon slowly rose across from her as she did the same. From the corner of her eye she could see Grizzly, and Grizzly appeared to be mirroring them, for it too was slowly rising. Artemis considered nocking an arrow, but decided that far too many animals had already been maimed since her arrival on Earth, and that karma would eventually get around to paying her a visit as it was without adding to the tally.

"Two..."

Artemis slipped out from under the table as if she were liquid; Poseidon slipped out from under the table as if he were made of coat-hangers. But at least they were slipping out from under the table, which was a good place to start.

Poseidon picked up his trident and, from the corner of his mouth, whispered, "Is it looking at us?"

Artemis nodded slowly. "Not only that," she said, "but it appears to be readying itself for a sprint. No! Don't look. You'll only make it worse." Slowly, very slowly, they edged away from the table. Poseidon, for some strange reason, began to tiptoe. "Three!" Artemis said, which appeared to come as quite a shock to Poseidon, despite three always coming next in the sequence[1].

They ran for the door—an old man and a Girl Guide, leaving without settling the bill—and Grizzly bolted after them, knocking diners sideways as it went. Its bark was so loud, ten people in the near-vicinity dropped down dead of fright[2].

Artemis was about to throw the door open when it opened of its own accord. Behind her, but only just, Poseidon lowered his trident. What was the point in having godly powers if you couldn't splurge every now and again? One of the perks of being a God was opening doors before you got to them. Another perk was all the grapes people kept forcing into your mouth when you weren't looking. Poseidon was sure there was a third perk, but he was too busy running to remember it.

They were out on the street now, careening across the pavement, dodging humans left, right, and centre.

---

[1] If she had said twelvety-two, his surprised expression would have been warranted.

[2] Had they not been on their way to make a complaint to the CEO of Dodge & E. Pacemakers Ltd., things might have been very different.

Artemis made the mistake of glancing across her shoulder, and then across Poseidon's shoulder, for Grizzly was in hot pursuit, its tongue flapping about in the wind and rain, its odd-shaped head bouncing up and down as it ran.

Artemis reached a corner and turned right. Poseidon did the same.

"Why don't we fly?" he called after Artemis, slightly out of breath, which was a very good question. It was the kind of question that would make you go, "Not sure," before breaking into laughter at the sheer stupidity.

"I can't!" Artemis said. "Not on a full stomach."

"You had three toilet breaks!"

"Yes, but one of them was a phantom," she said as they emerged onto another street.

"Oh," said Poseidon.

"Brrrrroooooff!" said Grizzly.

"On the bright side," Artemis said, "at least we're immortal." Of course, being immortal did not mean that they could not feel pain. They felt it just the same as everyone else. The only difference was that they didn't whinge about it. If Grizzly caught up to them—which it would eventually—and began to tear strips from them—which seemed to be its objective—it would not kill them, but it wouldn't be pleasant. It wouldn't be pleasant forcing a finger into the poor mutt, either, in order to relax its jaw, but needs must.

"This way!" Artemis said.

She hoped it *was* this way.

*

Vinnie had been following a Girl Guide—and feeling generally wrong about it—for almost ten minutes when another one spilled out onto the street[1]. So, just another Girl Guide in a city seemingly teeming with them? Not quite, for this one, who was now running along the pavement as if her life depended on it, had a bow and a quiver of arrows strapped to her back.

Now Vinnie was not the sharpest tool in the drawer, nor even the second sharpest. In fact, in a drawer full of sharp things, Vinnie was a potato

---

[1] It is a proven fact that if you wait long enough, two buses, each with the same destination in mind, will arrive at the exact same time. Other things that come in twos are new car-keys, bookends, and Kit-Kat fingers. Oh, and Girl Guides.

masher. However, he knew an assassin disguised as a sweet little girl when he saw one, and post-haste proceeded to give chase.

"Why are *you* running?" a booming and breathless voice asked, and when Vinnie glanced to his left, he noticed the old man running alongside him. Dressed in a flowing white robe which fluttered behind him as he hurried inexorably forward. "Forgot to pay as well, did you?"

"Um," Vinnie said, for he hadn't a clue what to do.

This was clearly the man who he had been ordered to whack. Vinnie glanced down just to make sure, saw the sandals, and decided that, yes, there was no doubt about it. Though why he was carrying a big fork, Vinnie didn't know.

"Anyway, it was nice talking to you," said the man, before speeding ahead and leaving a tornado of litter and leaves in his wake.

"Hang on a minute!" Vinnie called, but it was no use. The old robed fella was simply too fast, for he had caught up with his Girl Guide companion and was now berating her for something or other. Vinnie was too far away to hear what.

Just then, something barked, and when Vinnie glanced back and saw the culprit, his heart leapt into his mouth and something that wasn't his heart leapt into his boxers. At first he thought it was a bear, but even the bluntest object in the drawer knows that bears are not indigenous to London. Something to do with the smog, perhaps, or an innate fear of Uber drivers.

No, this was a dog. A large dog. A large slobbering dog with a very loud bark. The kind of dog that belonged on a leash, with a muzzle, strapped to a piece of board on castors like Hannibal Lector.

It was in pursuit of the old man and the Girl Guide, and now, because he was going in the same direction and at almost the same pace, it was in pursuit of Vinnie, too, which didn't seem fair, but that's what you get when you decide to start running through London. If it wasn't a dog, it was a middle-Eastern woman carrying a rose and a solemn expression, and if it wasn't her it was a hippie rattling a charity tin and banging on about the plight of the penguins[1].

Up ahead there was a busy road. Cars darted across the intersection, their drivers clenching their eyes tightly shut and hoping for the best, which is, as daft as it sounds, the safest way to drive around London. The girl and the old man hurtled across the road, over car bonnets and, remarkably, under buses. The lights changed from red to green and a torrent of traffic from the other direction began to ease forward.

The dog was almost upon Vinnie now, and as a result he had started to make strange whining noises in his throat. He reached the busy road and, without stopping, continued across it, which was partly where he went wrong, because although the cars and vans and trucks and buses were at a halt, the cycling lane

---

[1] If you were to ask the penguins, they would say, "What plight? We're bloody loving life. Be nice to be able to fly, but apart from that we can't really complain... okay, one complaint. Whose idea was it to have Morgan Freeman narrate us? Everywhere we go, there's his voice. I mean, it's a lovely voice, don't get me wrong, but it's too calming, you see. Hard enough trying to stay away when all you've got to look at is snow and ice and other penguins, but throw Morgan Freeman's voice into the mix and you've got yourself a regular South Pole snoozefest."

was in full flow, which meant that arseholes in Day-Glo yellow jerseys were doing what they did best, and that was ignoring all rules of the road.

"Look out!" screamed one such arsehole a moment before slamming into Vinnie at forty-five-miles per hour.

Vinnie's whole life flashed before his eyes, which was time, he could not help thinking, that would be better spent rolling into a ball and preparing to hit the tarmac on the other side of the junction. Still, he watched as his life play out before him, mainly because there wasn't anything else on.

Here he was roughing up some fat kid over a packet of Panini stickers. Vinnie remembered it like it was yesterday, and it had been, for he had had time to kill before meeting Spinelli at the club, and the kid was just there in the middle of the street with is FIFA '17 album open, peeling the back from a foil LFC crest. Asking for trouble, Vinnie had thought at the time.

There he was eating an ice-cream at the seaside, though he didn't think that memory was one of his and quickly shooed it away like a recalcitrant beagle.

Here he was standing in front of a mirror, his first gangster suit hanging off him like it was his inaugural day at Big School. "You look like a gangster!" his mother had exclaimed, almost dropping her tea and a plate of digestives as she entered the living-room. Although he wasn't sure that memory was real, either, or just a result of watching *Goodfellas* one too many times.

There he was—

Apparently, there was no more time for his life to flash before his eyes, and he skidded across the road like a hockey-puck, leaving skin and bits of flesh behind as he went. Car horns honked and people screamed; a middle-Eastern woman appeared in Vinnie's blurred vision and said, "Would you like to buy a rose for the lovely lady?" before she was ushered out of the way by Day-Glo Derek.

"Are you alright, mate?" said the cyclist. "You came out of nowhere."

Funny that, Vinnie thought, because so did you. He could not talk, though, because half his larynx had been ripped out and lay fifteen feet away. It didn't lie there long, as the bear-dog loped toward it, snuffled it up, and was gone as quick as you could say "Bad boy!"

Am I dying? Vinnie thought. Is this how I die? Run down by a would-be Bradley Wiggins? It was not how he had envisioned it. Gangsters don't get hit by bicycles; they get hit by their friends. They get blown up in their cars because it's all very cinematic. They get thrown in the Thames in suitcases, only to surface somewhere in Gloucester a few years later to frighten the life out of a WI walking group.

"Stay still, mate," said the cyclist.

"Hmph," Vinnie replied, which was not at all what he had intended. What he meant to say was, "Stay still? Stay fucking still? If I could bloody move I'd have bounced your head off the road by now. Stay still, indeed."

Off in the distance sirens dopplered through the streets. It would be another two hours before the ambulance arrived, for this was London and not some Disney fairy-tale. After five minutes of waiting, the cyclist made his apologies and left. Apparently, he was on his way to a wine-tasting event. "Don't want to miss the beginning," he had told Vinnie before scarpering. "They're opening a Casa Ferreirinha Barca Velha Douro 1938."

"Mph!" Vinnie had replied. *Prick.*

He lay there in the rain in the middle of the busy intersection, crippled by a bicycle and wondering whether the dog had enjoyed his larynx, watching the tyres of the cars as they steered cautiously around him, and cursing the emergency services for their failure to appear within ten seconds of the accident.

What do I pay my taxes for? he thought. Not that he paid his taxes, but that wasn't the point, the ambulance driver didn't know that, get a fucking wriggle on.

"Have you heard about the plight of the penguin?" a voice said, snapping Vinnie from his deathbed reverie. The sentence was punctuated by the rattle of a single tuppence in a charity collection tin. "Having to listen to Morgan Freeman all day, going on, and on, and on…"

Vinnie closed his eyes.

The sirens drew closer.

The penguin guy droned on.

"Would you like to buy a rose for the young lady?" a middle-Eastern voice said, to which the charity guy replied, "Only if you listen to me waffle on about the plight of the penguins for fifteen minutes before telling me you don't have any spare change and that you've never really gotten along with penguins anyway."

A deal was struck and off they went to annoy one another, leaving Vinnie in peace, and, sadly, also in pieces.

*

"Phew!" Artemis said, doubling over and clutching at her belly. She could just make out the faint sound of sloshing, of sausages sailing upon a stormy sea of coffee, of hash browns bobbing about the place like potato buoys, and don't even ask about the baked beans. "That was close," she said, wiping sweat from her brow and shaking her pigtails about like a wet dog. "Surprising how fast that thing can shift, given its size. Almost as quick as a sphinx, dare I say."

Poseidon paced back and forth along the pavement, shaking his head and muttering expletives under his breath.

"Are you okay?" Artemis asked.

"No, I bloody well am not!" Poseidon said. "We shouldn't be here, and we almost certainly shouldn't be drawing attention to ourselves."

"You're the one dressed like you're about to board an ark," Artemis said.

Poseidon lunged for her, his trident raised. Tiny thunderbolts danced around its tines and the faint sizzle of electricity could be heard if you put your head right next to it, which was a stupid thing to do.

"You will be the death of me, girl," he said as he brought the trident down hard upon the pavement, sending cracks spider-webbing out in all directions. "It is time for us to—"

"'Ello, 'ello, 'ello," said a voice. "What have we got here then, huh?"

The voice belonged to a man, and he approached them swinging what appeared to be some sort of beating aubergine. Upon his head sat a tall blue hat, and there were numbers strapped to his uniform which probably meant something, but for the life of her Artemis couldn't think what it might be.

As the strange man reached them—there was no reason to assume he was strange, but his clothes definitely suggested he was eccentric, and the way he swung his aubergine insinuated there was something not quite right about him—the box attached to his breast crackled and squawked. It wasn't a $\pi\sum\prod$ but, then again, even the humans have to draw the line somewhere.

"You do know that, under the Criminal Damage Act of 1971, it is an offence for any person to have anything in his custody or under his control, intending without lawful excuse to use it or cause or permit another to use it—"

"Are you some sort of Ephor?" Artemis said.

The man didn't seem to enjoy being interrupted, for he reached down to the squawking box, depressed the button[1], and said, "I'm going to need backup! I repeat, multiple suspects, one of which is carrying a big fork and the other looks like she's about to search

---

[1] He often depressed the button. The button had tried, unsuccessfully and on many occasions, to detach from the radio and lob itself in the Thames.

Hyde Park on the off-chance someone's lost an antelope!"

"Um," Poseidon said, taking the slightest of steps forward but then freezing as soon as the man raised his aubergine.

"Don't you move another muscle," said the man. "And you," he said to Artemis, "any more wisecracks or rude names from you, and I'll have no choice but to write a strongly-worded letter to my superintendent."

Artemis thought about explaining to the man what an Ephor was, that there was nothing derogatory about it, and that without Ephors, Greece wouldn't be the place it was today[1]. She thought about it, and then decided against it when two cars with flashing blue lights pulled up to the kerb, from which climbed more of the mad blue mystery men.

"We don't have time for this," Poseidon said out of

---

[1] $30 trillion in debt, not that anyone's counting any more. Like all debts, once you reach a certain point, you might as well go mental. Greece is over there right now, a stack of unpaid, unopened bills sitting on its kitchen table and wondering whether it was best to just make a run for it, change its name to Kevin, and hope no one notices.

the corner of his mouth.

"We don't even know what this is," Artemis replied in a likewise manner.

"These are *policemen*," Poseidon said. "It is their job to arrest us, transfer us kicking and screaming to a cold and filthy cell where they will proceed to rough us up until we confess to being terrorists."

"But we're not," Artemis said, watching as the four blue men formed a huddle.

"That does not matter to these men," Poseidon said, and then, "Take my hand and I will fly us out of here."

"I will do no such thing," Artemis said. "I would very much like to see how this plays out." She was having a blast. In fact, she hadn't had this much fun since The Trojan War.

"We are carrying—" Poseidon tapped a finger against the handle of his trident "—dangerous weapons. The humans do not like it when people waltz through their city, armed to the back teeth. It makes them nervous."

"My bow is for hunting and self-defence," Artemis

said. The blue men were writing things in their little notepads now and eyeing Artemis and Poseidon with no small amount of wariness.

"We can leave," Poseidon said. "Right now. We leave, and we do not look back."

Artemis shook her head. They could not simply take to the skies and expect to get away with it, for they had four witnesses. And if they were, indeed, 'Polis Men' like Poseidon said, it was only right to expect they had access to flying machines and the like.

The blue man that had initially stopped them stepped forwards, his eyebrows knitted together as he gnawed upon his bottom lip as if he didn't like it half as much as the top one and would be much happier once it was gone. "There are two ways we can do this," he said.

"I'm sure there are a lot more than two ways," Artemis said. "Now, if you'd said there are an infinite number of ways we can do this—"

"The first way," the blue man interrupted, "is we take your illegal weaponry, throw you in the back of that vehicle over there, transport you to the station, check you in, and then proceed to rough you up until you tell us what we want to hear, by which time we'll no doubt be knackered and accept what you have to say as gospel and then release you while we stand at the desk sergeant's desk, muttering amongst ourselves and discussing Breaking Bad."

Artemis did not like the sound of that one bit. "What is the second option?"

"On-the-spot fine," said the blue man.

"Neither of us has any money," Poseidon said, turning the pockets of his robe out to prove it.

"That's okay," said the blue man, producing a small booklet from his pocket and scribbling upon it. "You have twenty-eight days to pay. If you fail to do so, see option one."

"Seems fair," Artemis said. She moved slowly across to the blue man, glanced across his shoulder as he wrote up the ticket, and said, "My name is Ares and my address is number 1, Mount Olympus."

15

It was a miserable day in the city. Rain came down in sheets, and soggy hobos wandered aimlessly about the place like lost lambs. And on top of all that, Simian had the worst headache ever. So bad was this headache that his face was all scrunched up. He looked like someone who sucked lemons for a living[1].

He walked around the edge of Stepney Green Park, dodging puddles as if they were molten lava and occasionally stopping to straighten his face, for people were looking at him funny and giving him a wide berth.

An hour ago he had been spark out on his office carpet, a carpet which now looked as if a gang of hippies had arrived in the dead of night and started a fire upon it so that they had something to sing Kumbaya around.

The strange woman with the golden glow had been real; Simian knew that now. What he did not know was how she happened to be there. Or the one with the bow, or the one with the great big bloody fork. It had not been a dream, and he was not going mad.

---

[1] Although not the best job in the world, it beat sucking socks.

Something very strange was going on, and he—

"Rose for the beautiful lady?" said a middle-Eastern voice, which fairly threw Simian off his train of thought. He turned to find a woman, standing no higher than his nipples, thrusting a rose toward him as if it were a grenade and she wanted nothing more to do with it. She had a kind smile, but so did Hitler when he wanted something.

"I'm sorry," Simian said, squinting through the rain. "I don't have a beautiful lady."

"Awwww," said the woman, which was either genuine or sarcastic as fuck. "Rose for the beautiful man?"

"I don't have one of those either," Simian said, riffling around in his pocket for something to make the woman go away. "Here's ten pence—" he pulled the coin from his pocket and flicked it in her general direction "—and I'd appreciate it if you didn't pop up anymore, especially when I'm deep in thought and a million miles away."

The woman thanked him profusely which, unfortunately, involved tongues, and as she dashed away Simian made a mental note to get himself checked over at the next available opportunity.

Ten minutes later he arrived at his destination. It looked a lot different from this angle, without thorns in front of his face and with the shutters up. Through the large glass frontage, he watched the beautiful redhead dip things in batter and then throw them under the halogen heat-lamps, where they would spend the rest of the day fending off flies and looking all forlorn and needy.

A big guy wearing a filthy white apron went to work on a rotating slab of doner meat as if it had said something to offend him. That must be Harry, Simian thought. But he wasn't here to see Harry; he was here for the redhead, the dame who would probably lead to trouble, as they so often did.

He walked toward the chippie, pushed open the door, and headed for the counter.

"We're not open yet," said the redhead without looking up from a lugubrious Dover sole. "Come back in about an hour—"

"," Simian said, putting his hands on the stainless-steel counter. "Ferfucksake!" he said, taking his hands off the stainless-steel counter and leaving his palms behind. "You should put a sign up—"

Still focussing on the fish, the redhead motioned to the tiled wall to Simian's left, upon which was Sellotaped a piece of paper with three words printed upon it in Comic Sans. HOT COUNTER, IDIOT!

"Well," Simian said, blowing at his palms and wondering how long it would take for his fingerprints to grow back, "you need to make it more visible."

"I'll bear that in mind," said the redhead as she turned away from the counter and pretended to occupy herself with the till. After a few moments, once she'd polished all the buttons and replaced the receipt roll three times, she said, "Look, I can't serve you until after eleven—" and that was when she turned and looked at Simian for the first time since his arrival, and it was a look of abject horror.

Simian quickly straightened his face and said, "Don't be alarmed. I just want to talk to you about what happened last night."

"Is this man bothering you, Margot?" said Harry,

turning away from his doner meat but leaving his little handsaw running. He looked like something from a low-budget horror movie. *The Doner-Meat Massacre*, coming soon to a chip-shop near you, rated 18 for extended scenes of battery[1] and the occasional dropped polystyrene tub of curry sauce.

"Look, I don't want any trouble," Simian said, and he leaned nonchalantly upon the counter as if to prove how much trouble he didn't want. "Ferfucksake!" He pulled his arms and fingered at the smouldering holes in his trench-coat. "The sign should be on the counter!" he hissed.

"It's okay, Barry," said the redhead, which was odd because his name was Harry, Simian thought. "I'll be two minutes." She removed her apron and walked to the end of the counter, where there was one of those lifty-uppy jobbies.

Simian went outside and the redhead followed. Once the door had shut—it took almost a whole minute as it was on a hydraulic hinge—Simian turned to the woman and said, "I'm not here to discuss your

---

[1] Ahem.

affair with Jack Spinelli. What you do in your own time is none of my business—"

"Which explains why you were hiding in that bush last night, taking pictures," she said.

"Yes, well, um," Simian said. "I'm a private investigator, you see, and hiding in bushes is what I do for a living. Very occasionally I have intercourse with a beautiful dame, but those occurrences are few and far between."

"What do you want?" the redhead said, clearly not falling for his charms. Perhaps it was because of his screwed-up face. Damn you, headache!

"I want to know what went on here last night," he said. "I don't remember much of it."

"Oh, yes, that's right," she said. "You were over there in the bushes with a vacant look on your face. Life flash before your eyes, did it?"

"It did, actually," Simian said. "But that's beside the point. I was shot by someone, and I was wondering if you could fill in the gaps."

"I thought they were with you," she said.

"Excuse me?"

"The bloke in the robe and his little archer friend. I thought they were with you."

Simian shook his head. "If they were with me," he said, "why would one of them put an arrow through my shoulder?"

Judging by the redhead's expression, she thought that was a damn good question. "It takes all sorts," she said, as if that explained everything and they could both go home, safe in the knowledge that she had sorted the problem out, and you're very welcome.

"I haven't a clue who they were," Simian said with a shrug. "And if they're not on your boyfriend's payroll, then there's someone going around the city, indiscriminately shooting people in the shoulders with arrows, which, by the way, there should be a law against."

"I believe there is," said the redhead. "Under sections 18 and 20 of the Offences against the persons act 1981—"

"You just made that up," Simian said. "Stop it."

The redhead—whose name, according to Harry Ramsden, was Margot something-or-other—lit a cigarette, offered one to Simian, which he gladly took, and said, "Things are not what they seem," which was a very strange thing for her to say, but Simian decided to let her get on with it. But what she said next was the straw that broke the camel's back, the icing on the proverbial cake, and the *coup de grace* all rolled into one. "You are Simian Knight PI of 231 Camomile House. You like to live dangerously, which is why you leave the utility bills until the day before you're due to be cut off before paying them. You once had a mother, and some say, even a father, and you like nothing more than fornicating with a beautiful dame, when the opportunity presents itself."

"—" Simian said, which was about all he could manage.

"You were once shot at, although that might be something of an exaggeration, and your favourite member of the Spice Girls is Baby, because there's something oddly innocent about her compared to the others, and rabbits-in-the-headlights are right up your back-alleyway."

"Um," Simian said, scratching at his sore head. *Um,*

he thought, is better than nothing.

"Due to the monochromatic nature of your world, you have never seen the colour cerise, and if you did you would simply write it off as just another pink, hardly worthy of its own special name." She took a pull on her cigarette before continuing. "You relish long-fought battles against the city skyline with evil villains, but only because you've never actually had one and it would be nice to see what all the fuss is about."

Simian lit a cigarette of his own, for he was a firm believer in the old adage 'if you can't beat them, join them', and also the new adage, 'if you can't talk because you're beyond impressed by the wealth of knowledge pouring from a chip-shop worker, join them'.

"You've always wondered how people stay afloat in water, and even took up swimming classes for a time in order to unravel the mystery, but once resuscitated you decided to forget all about it and concentrate on staying on dry land instead. You have two sisters, both of whom are estranged due to the nature of your business."

"And what is the nature of my business?" Simian

asked, finally finding his voice once again.

"Other people's business," the redhead said. "Like most private investigators, you have no soul and simply exist to pile misery upon others—"

"Now hang on a minute—"

"but not before extracting as much money as possible from those very same people. You, Mr Knight, are the lowest of the low."

"I will not tolerate th—"

"You will," said the redhead, "because I haven't finished with you just yet." She flicked her cigarette butt at the ground; sparks flew everywhere, including into Simian's shoe. She waited for him to finish dancing before going on. "Forget whatever it is Stella Spinelli has asked you to do."

"Oh, you'd like that, wouldn't you," Simian said. "What's the matter? Don't like sharing?"

Two things happened then, both of which came as quite a shock to Simian. Firstly, Harry pushed open the shop door and tossed a vat of old batter out onto the street; if Simian hadn't known better, he could have sworn it was meant for him. Fortunately, he had his wits about him and dodged the batter just in time.

And secondly, the beautiful redhead whipped out a badge and said, "I operate undercover for the Met. We've been working on Spinelli for almost three years, and we're a gnat's fart away from getting what we need, so just forget all about him, tell Stella Spinelli you don't know anything and that you can't take her money, and take a little holiday to the Maldives until this all blows over."

Simian was flabbergasted. Not only that but he was dumbstruck, astonished, and a little flummoxed.

"You really shouldn't let your face do that," said the redhead. "If a fly gets in there you'll know about it."

"You're a cop?" Simian said. "An undercover cop?"

This made the redhead smile. "You didn't think this whole thing was going to play out with no strong female characters, did you?" Simian's silence said that, yes, that was pretty much how it worked, and that changing the formula now would be like drafting in a beautiful actress to play Doctor Who[1], thusly giving

---

[1] Whatever next? A female Wonder Woman? A female Erin Brockovich? A man dressed up as a giant lizard? Two eight-

him his first time-travelling crush since William Hartnell[1]. "What are you? A caveman?"

"You've just taken me by surprised," he said, examining the badge in her hand as if it were some sort of magnificent forgery. "Are you sure you're not just pulling my leg?"

"I think I would know if that were the case," she said. "And what might shock you even more is that my real name is not, in fact, Margot Trix."

"Get the fuck out of here!" Simian said. A bit of spittle landed on the redhead's lip, and he tried not to draw attention to it, but he knew that she knew it was there. They always know it's there. "What's your name, then?"

"I'm afraid I can't disclose that information," she said, which was precisely what one might expect to be told by an undercover agent. "In fact, I've already told

---

year-olds Sellotaped together to play Malcolm X? I could go on, but I won't.

[1] There is, according to Simian, something about William Hartnell, a little *je ne sais quoi* that he can't quite put his finger on, but which most probably has something to do with the hair.

you too much. As far as you're concerned, my name is Margot Trix and I work at Harry Ramsden's. Got it?"

The thing was, five minutes ago he would have accepted that without question. But now that he had seen the badge, and had spoken to the redhead at length, it was hard to think of her as anything other than an undercover agent for the Met. "Got it," he said, although he hadn't, and besides he needed the money Stella Spinelli had paid him for such luxuries as keeping the lights on, keeping the heating on, and, most importantly, keeping his weight on. "I have a small question," he added, in an effort to keep the conversation flowing, more than anything.

"Hurry up," Margot said, glancing across her shoulder to the chip shop. "I've got solemn fish to batter."

"Why a chip shop?" Simian said. "I always thought undercover agents did cool things, like pose as international car thieves, or infiltrate gangs by pretending to be good at computer stuff, just in case the head of the gang was having trouble hacking into things."

"We had it on good authority that Jack Spinelli doesn't like to shit on his own doorstep."

Simian nodded. "Who does?" he said.

"So it was decided that I would assume the role of a chip shop worker, albeit a beautiful one."

"You're doing quite a good job of it."

"And, it just so turns out, that Spinelli has an insatiable appetite when it comes to mushy pea fritters."

"Good for him."

"Things are moving along nicely. Spinelli's already starting to open up about his business associates, the deals he and the other mob families have in place, and how many people he's stuffed in suitcases and tossed into the Thames. We're almost ready to make a move on him, so I would really appreciate it if you skedaddled and tried not to get yourself in any deeper than you already are, lest you find yourself folded over like a pair of novelty pyjamas and rammed into a fifteen-inch item of holiday baggage."

Simian didn't like the sound of that, but he also didn't like the thought of not being paid. On the other hand, if Spinelli was under surveillance, and was about to be pounced upon by various agencies, didn't it make sense to stand back and let them do all the legwork? Besides, the whole job was a sham. If Spinelli wasn't really cheating, which he wasn't because the other half of the relationship wasn't who she said she was, would it stand up in a divorce court? Simian doubted it, which meant that Stella would not be granted access to half of Spinelli's assets. Even worse than that, she would have to remain married to him for the entire duration of his incarceration.

"How long do you think he'll get?" Simian said.

"Well," Margot replied, and took a deep breath, which was never a good sign. "There are fifteen counts of money laundering, twenty-two murders, a dozen or so counts of kidnapping, one-hundred-and-fifteen counts of arson, twenty-eight counts of GBH, eleven counts of supplying firearms, three unpaid parking tickets, and one count of smoking in front of a no-smoking sign." She took another deep breath. "Needless to say, it's a good job he doesn't have any grandchildren."

"Because they wouldn't see him until they were adults?"

"No, I just don't like grandchildren," said Margot. "But, to answer your question, I haven't a clue how long they're going to put him away for. If the judge wakes up on the morning of the trial to a nice breakfast, followed by a brief but satisfying bout of sex with his wife, and provided there's no traffic on the way to the courthouse, Spinelli's probably looking at ten life sentences, to be served consecutively."

Simian whistled, which was a shame as he wasn't very good at it.

"If the judge hits traffic, I'd say he's looking at a death sentence."

"We don't have that in this country," Simian said. "Not last time I looked."

"Trust me," Margot said, which was a ridiculous thing for an undercover agent to say, "they're thinking of bringing it back just for Spinelli. It'll be a one-off, probably, but if all goes well..." She crossed her fingers and smiled evilly.

"Margot!" Harry stood between the doorframe

with pieces of kebab meat draped across his shoulders like some half-arsed Lady GaGa.

"Coming, Barry," Margot told him. She turned back to Simian and gave him a little wink[1]. "Forget about everything I've told you," she said. "And please, please, for the sake of national security, keep your beak out."

She turned and rushed toward the chip shop, leaving Simian standing out in the drizzle, his entire world turned upside down by a redheaded dame in a filthy white apron.

Five minutes later, he was on his way to the local carpet shop.

---

[1] Only a little one, but it was enough.

16

There are very few carpet shops on Mount Olympus. Sure, at the market you can't move for rugs. Rugs and doormats. Upon the doormats are printed such Greek witticisms as καλως ΗΡΘΑΤΕ, roughly translated as WELCOME, and Δεν επιτρέπονται σανδάλια, or, as they say in England, NO SANDALS ALLOWED. But rugs and mats are no good when you've got ten bedrooms and a hall-stairs-and-landing to carpet, not to mention Pantheon and Zeus's throne room. It would cost a fortune to carpet the whole thing, which is why much of the Olympians' headquarters is covered with lino.

Zeus had walked across the lino so many times that there was now a slight track. "I have no choice, Hera, but to call a meeting," he said.

Hera was sitting at the giant twelve-deity table with a bowl of cornflakes. "If you think it will help," she said, in a tone that suggested she didn't.

Hovering over the table, rotating slowly and occasionally blinking out of existence thanks to the shitty Wi-Fi, was a holographic map of the Earth. If you looked really close you could see your house, although it had been a while since the Google Earth people had been around to update it so you would most probably also see the previous owner's car sitting on the drive, along with the roundabout at the bottom of the street which is no longer there, and the beautiful green field a couple of streets away which is now a Londis.

"I can't stand idly by while Artemis makes a fool out of me," Zeus said, clutching his thunderbolt so tightly that sparks were flying. "We need to come up with a plan."

"Poseidon almost has her home," Hera said, turning the page of her Woman's Weekly and wiping milk from her chin. "Just a few more hours and it will all be over."

Zeus dropped down into his seat at the head of the table. "That's easy for you to say."

"It was," Hera said. "However, I struggle enormously with onomatopoeia." She looked shocked for a moment. It was a miracle!

"I simply cannot allow this to go on for another few minutes, let alone a few hours." Zeus pushed a red button on his end of the table and began to speak.

"Children, this is your five-minute-warning. I expect you all to join us in the meeting room presently. We have urgent matters to discuss."

"Tell them there will be chocolate fudge cookies," Hera said, pushing her empty bowl away and getting stuck in to a magazine quiz which would tell her which Greek goddess she would be, if such a thing were possible.

"Your mother says there will be hot fudge cookies," Zeus said. "And also, if you're not here by the time the holographic Earth completes one rotation, you're all grounded and I'm confiscating all your gems and treasures until such a time as I see fit to return them to you." He released the red button and settled back in his chair.

"Don't be so hard on them," Hera muttered without looking up. "It's not their fault Artemis has been stricken by wanderlust."

Zeus grunted. "They're all as bad as one another," he said. "I've given them everything, up to and including the keys to the universe, and how do they repay me? I knew I should have stopped at three children, but no, you wanted a football team, didn't you, and to hell with the consequences." He set his thunderbolt down on the table and gave it a little spin. "Hades had the right idea—"

"Will you stop bringing up that maniac while I'm breakfasting," Hera said.

"At least he stopped at two children," Zeus went on. "And do you know what he got instead of a third child? A vasectomy and a three-headed dog." He paused and gave the thunderbolt another spin. "I'd kill for a three-headed dog."

"Do you have any idea how much upkeep that would be?" Hera said. "And besides, it's not just a three-headed dog, is it? It's got bits of snake sticking out of it, and you know how much I despise snakes. Ever since that Medusa—"

"I knew this was about Medusa!" Zeus said. "I can't have a three-headed dog because—"

"You can't have a three-headed dog," Hera said, "because the novelty wears off with you. If you get a three-headed dog, a week later you'll want a four-headed dog. And then when you're bored of that, you'll want a talking hamster."

"I won't," Zeus said.

"We're not getting a three-headed dog," Hera said. "Hades can afford one, on account of all the kids he doesn't have."

Zeus huffed and gave his thunderbolt a third spin. It crackled and hissed as it went, but you wouldn't know that because Zeus's huff drowned it out. After a few seconds, he pushed the red button again and said, "Ten… nine… eight…"

Gods and goddesses began to pile into the room.

First came Hephaestus, perhaps the ugliest of Zeus's children. But what he lacked in beauty he more than made up for with craftmanship. Hephaestus could fix anything with a blob of blu-tack and a paperclip, but despite the ease with which he fixed things, he always left an extortionate invoice.

Aphrodite was next and looking as beautiful as ever. Even with bed-head she made every other woman in the universe look as if they'd just been dragged through a hedge backwards[1].

Apollo, Athena, and Demeter appeared in the room and took their seats, as did Hermes, Dionysus, and Hestia. As if Zeus wasn't sat at the end of the table, angrily spinning his thunderbolt and huffing like a bull in a china shop, Hermes proceeded to tell Dionysus and Hestia a joke. "So Zeus, right," he said with a huge smile. "Zeus is flying over Greece, yeah, and he looks down, and there, lying stark-bollock naked on a beach, is this beautiful woman, right?" Everyone was listening now, including Zeus. "So Zeus flies down and goes, hey, I'm Zeus, God of Thunder, Ruler of the Olympians, yada, yada, yada."

Little snickers around the table.

"So the woman falls instantly in love with him. Because, you know, Ruler of the Olympians has a nice ring to it and whatnot. So they do it right there on the beach. It goes on for like, thirty seconds, I don't know how long Zeus goes for, right? And at the end of it,

---

[1] Presumably, if you were to drag a person through a hedge forwards they would look as beautiful as Aphrodite, but no one has ever tried it so it's all conjecture, really.

they're spent and just lying there looking up at the sun, sand in all their cracks, and Zeus says, 'In nine months you will have a child, and you will call him Hercules'."

"Stupid name," Apollo said.

"Ridiculous," added Hestia.

"Then," Hermes said, "the woman turns to Zeus, and she says, 'In nine days, you will have a rash and you will call it Herpes."

The whole table, minus Zeus, erupted with laughter. Hera's cereal bowl leapt from the table and smashed into a hundred pieces on the lino, and it took several seconds for everyone to catch their breaths.

"Yes, very funny," Zeus said, once the din had died down enough to be heard. "Herpes, of course, because we should all make fun of people inflicted with sexually-transmitted-diseases." There was no humour in his voice, mostly because he didn't find anything humorous about Hermes' joke. "Okay, now that we've all got that out of our systems, can we concentrate on the matter at hand?"

"Tell us another one, Hermes," Dionysus said.

Hermes grinned. "A priest, a whore, and Zeus walk

into a bar—"

"Silence!" Zeus said, angrily snatching his thunderbolt up from the table. "This isn't the Glee Club, you bunch of clowns! This is Mount Olympus! I will not have it turned into some sort of... some sort of joke factory."

All around the table the gods shrank into their seats, and it was at this point that Zeus realised there were now *three* empty chairs.

"Okay," he said, glancing about the room. "who's missing."

"Artemis," Aphrodite said. "And Poseidon."

"They've been missing since yesterday," Athena said to Zeus. "Perhaps you should have a little lie down. The stress must be getting to you."

"I know," Zeus said, "that Artemis and Poseidon are absent, but the person who sits in that chair there—" and he pointed toward it "—is also not here, hence the reason why it is empty."

The Olympians looked at one another, then looked at Hera, before reluctantly looking at Zeus again.

"Ares," Apollo said. "That's where Ares normally

sits. And since he is not there, might I be so bold as to suggest he is somewhere else?"

Zeus pushed the red button and said, "Ares, if you're not here in three seconds, I'm going to confiscate all your swords, all your shields, and that strange little catapult thing you like to shoot Mermen with.

"Three…"

"Two…"

"One-and-a-half…"

"One…"

"A half of one…"

But still the door to the meeting room remained shut, although now nine Olympians were staring at it, which probably didn't help. A shut door is very much like a boiling pot, or something.

"Well this is bloody ridiculous," Zeus said.

"Someone said there would be cookies," Hermes said, glancing about the table and seeing that there was no such thing.

"Start without him," Hera said. "You know what he's like, Zeus. He's probably up in his room, playing with his soldiers and sulking."

"What is the point of having a red button that summons gods," Zeus said, "if half the time, the gods don't pay any attention to it?"

"I *told* you the red button was a bad idea," Hera said, turning the page of her magazine. "But you were all, 'Hades has a red button, *I* want a red button'. And now that you've got one, and people are ignoring it, you're all, 'This red button doesn't work. I'll have to get a green button instead, at least—"

"Have you quite finished?" Zeus said.

Hera nodded that she had, then drew an invisible zip across her lips.

"Right," Zeus said. "Can one of you, I don't care which, go to Ares' room and fetch him. Tell him we're having a very important meeting, and his attendance is required, nay, compulsory."

Apollo sighed and stood. "I'll go," he said, "but if he's in a foul mood, and I take a spear to the throat, I want you all to remember this moment, for it was the moment I heroically volunteered—"

"Just piss off," Zeus said, "before I have to put my

slipper up your arse."

Apollo did as he was told and, once he was out of the room, Zeus decided to call a start to the meeting.

He turned the holographic globe with one hand until the United Kingdom was visible, and then zoomed in using his other hand. Operating the globe was a little like playing a theremin, only without the suffering that came with listening to a theremin being played.

Just then, the hologram flickered and a HTTP 404 ERROR NOT FOUND message popped up above it.

"Fucksticks!" Zeus said.

"Try reloading it," Hephaestus said. "If that doesn't work, I'll fetch my blu-tack."

Zeus reloaded the page, and sighed with relief when the 404 ERROR disappeared and the holographic globe resumed its perpetual rotating. He located London on the map, zoomed in to Stepney, then zoomed straight back out again when he saw, upon the screen, a man throwing up in the back of a taxi-cab. "Ah," he said. "Zoomed a little bit too much." He pulled out a bit, and then set about fiddling with the interface to the right of the hologram.

"This morning," he said, trying to keep the attention of those seated around the table, "at around ten o'clock GMT, Artemis and Poseidon were almost picked up by the authorities."

"What, like Ephors?" Aphrodite said.

"Something like that," Hera said. "On Earth they have things called 'policemen', and these 'policemen' have the authority to detain, incarcerate, and, if necessary, rough up a human until they smell colours and see sounds."

"Delightful!" Hermes said. "I should very much like to meet one."

"Ah!" Zeus said. "Here it is." And he hit PLAY.

A 3D holographic re-enactment of Artemis and Poseidon's run-in with the law played out for the Olympians. It was only interrupted once, when Hermes asked why the 'policeman' appeared to be carrying an aubergine, to which Zeus replied, "Fucked if I know."

Silence descended upon the meeting room, which was a first, as Artemis interacted with the 'policeman' as if she were normal, a mortal, a human. Why she didn't just put an arrow through the 'policeman' was anybody's guess.

The Olympians watched as Artemis gave the 'policeman' Ares' details, told them that if it wasn't paid within the allotted time, send SWAT, and don't stop shooting until the whole mountain looks like a cheese-grater.

Zeus was grateful Ares wasn't present to hear that part, for it would have sent him on the rampage, and the last thing they needed now was another loose cannon.

Once the playback was over, Zeus minimised the hologram, behind which was a screensaver, ZEUS IS IMPOTENT, which bounced around in thin air for a few moments before he realised what it said, for one of the little bastards had hacked into the system and fiddled with the settings. What it should have said was ZEUS IS OMNIPOTENT.

There were muted sniggers as Zeus quickly shut down the screensaver, logged off from the system entirely, and, in something of a fluster, relaxed back in his chair. "Very funny," he grunted, which it wasn't.

"So where are they now?" Hermes said, once he'd composed himself.

"Well," said Zeus, "that is the thing. They appear to have, as they say in the military, gone A.W.O.L. The system can no longer track them, thanks to unserviceable Wi-Fi. We have never been more blind. If I did not know better, I would say someone is sabotaging our efforts to retrieve our fellow Olympians."

"You're reading too much into it," Hera said, glancing momentarily up from her magazine. "Why would anyone want to prevent us from getting Artemis and Poseidon back safe and sound? It doesn't make any sense."

Just then, and seemingly at the perfect moment, Apollo rushed back into the room, his eyes wide and his mouth even wider. In his hand he clenched what appeared to be a small piece of paper. "He's gone!" he said. "Ares... Ares has gone!"

Zeus stood, so slowly and dramatically that if Michael Bay had been present, he would have captured the whole thing on camera and marketed it to the easily-entranced masses. "You're shitting me!" he said, which is probably where Michael Bay would have stopped filming.

"I wish I was," Apollo said. "But look! He even left a note, and, well, you're not going to like what he's done." He cleared his throat, as if he was best man at a wedding reception and was about to rip seven shades of shit out of an unwitting groom. With the page at arm's length, he began.

"My fellow Olympians. It is with great sadness that this day has arrived, for I always thought it would happen on a Tuesday, and it's Thursday today. Needless to say, things have gone tits-up and I've fairly had enough of it. I have therefore decided to ignore Father's pleas to avoid Earth like the proverbial plague, as I believe it is my duty to partake in battles, to start wars, and to stir shit up. If not for the fact it was my birthday last month, for which I received the disappointing gifts of an annual pass to the local Odeon and a pair of sandals, I would have done this earlier.

"I left early this morning, and do not believe I shall ever set foot upon Olympus again. If anyone wants my CD collection—and I'm talking primarily to Apollo here, as he also enjoys the work of Megadeth—then feel free to take it with my permission.

"You will notice, and Hera will be pleased to find, that my room is now somewhat cleaner. This is because I have taken with me very little in the way of clothes, but a lot in the way of spears, daggers, swords, shields, and catapults. I have also taken my horse, Shadow, from the outhouse, for he has always served me well and I don't trust the horses in London as far as I can throw them.

"I must state that, although it might seem like it, none of this is personal. Except, perhaps, for the screensaver I left for Father to find hiding behind the holographic globe." At this point Apollo paused, confusion etched across his face. Zeus waved him impatiently on. "Now this is where things get a little technical, so bear with me.

"You will not be able to follow me, for I have made a deal with Uncle Hades. Did you know he has a three-headed dog now? How cool is that? Anyway, I digress. Hades has taken Mount Olympus and hurled it out into the void. If you look out of your window, you will find the view most disconcerting."

Zeus marched across to the window, saw the view, found it most disconcerting, and then upchucked upon his own sandaled feet. Everything was... black. There was nothing out there, which was probably why the called it the void. "This is preposterous!" he said, wiping drool from his beard. "How *dare* Hades get involved in Olympian affairs." He looked out of the window again and said, "I haven't a bloody clue where we are."

"There's more," Apollo said.

Hera was up now, clutching onto Zeus as if he were a designer handbag. She looked terrified. In fact, they all did. Being cast into the void had that effect on people, gods or otherwise.

"I am not a complete bastard, and so the void has been ordered to spit you back out in a century or so, by which time Earth should be suitably destroyed. Well, except for those weird little microscopic creatures that look like socks with legs. Those'll probably still be knocking about the place, but nothing else."

"It is the ramblings of a madman!" Zeus said. "He'll never get away with this!"

Apollo went on. "I know it sounds as if I have lost my mind, and I know Father will probably be standing there right now, one arm wrapped around Hera and the other around his precious thunderbolt, yelling at the top of his voice about how I'll never get away with this—"

"Fair play," Zeus said.

"—but I can assure you that I *will* get away with it, and that I am *not* mad, at least I wasn't the last time I spoke to the voices in my head. It is time for a new Ruler of the Olympians, and a new Ruler of Earth.

"I am just the God for the job.

"Adios, suckers

"Ares.

"P.S. This piece of paper will set fire to itself in three seconds' time."

Apollo looked around at the faces of his brother, his

sisters, and his father, by which time the paper had burst into flames and he had no choice but to drop it and stamp on it several times, which would have been fine had he not been wearing sandals.

"This can't be happening," Hera said. "It all seems so… so far-fetched."

Zeus released his wife and turned to face the window once more. "It is happening," he said. "Which means only one thing."

"What?"

"We're in a whole heap of shit."

17

It is unusual to see a man on horseback in London. So unusual that people tend to stop and point and say things like, "Look at that man on horseback." Children's faces light up, as the image conjures up all sorts of amazing things. If you had a fiver for every time you saw a man on horseback sitting in traffic, you'd have a fiver and not a penny more.

Ares wasn't inclined to sit in traffic all day, and so he took to the pavement, Shadow whinnying beneath him, which elicited an altogether different response from the people of London, much of which involved the word, "Prick."

He rode on, ignoring the flashing blue lights and shrill sirens which appeared to be following him, for he had places to go and people to see.

Never before had he felt so alive.

*

"Never before have I felt so alive!" Artemis said, shrugging Poseidon off for the umpteenth time. "I'm not ready to go back to Olympus. At least let us stay for tea. I hear there's a diner in Camden which serves only raw chicken. Imagine that."

"No!" Poseidon said. "This has gone on long enough. Zeus is relying upon me to bring you home, and I will not let him down."

Artemis put some distance between herself and Poseidon and said, "I thought you were cool. I thought you were fun. But you're not fun, are you? You're just as bad as Zeus."

Poseidon sighed. "If it were up to me, you would be allowed to remain here forever, amongst the humans and free to do whatever you like, but it is not my choice." He gave her a little poke with his trident. "I have no choice, Artemis. We must return to Olympus, for we are gods, and these people are… well, they are not."

Artemis sulked. She sulked and she brooded, all the while trying to find fault in Poseidon's logic. After almost two minutes of moping and pouting, she concluded, somewhat reluctantly, that Poseidon was right. Earth belonged to the mortals. It was time to go home.

"Fine!" she said, folding her arms across her chest.

"We'll go, if that's what you really want."

Poseidon smiled a little. "That is what I want," he said. "Let us return to our castle in the clouds, for we have pretty much fucked up our short time here on Earth. It is time to begin anew, and I promise I will not allow Zeus to reproach you for this. You are young and wish to see things. He is old, and has probably already seen everything there is to see at least twice."

Artemis smiled. "I do not fear Zeus's wrath," she said, even though she did. "His thunderbolt does not frighten me." It was what he could do with it which frightened her. On its own, Zeus's thunderbolt was nothing more than a novelty night-light; in her Father's hands it had the power to end worlds, to destroy universes, and also to stir a cup of tea whilst at the same time bringing it up to a drinkable temperature.

"Ready?" Poseidon said, thrusting his free hand into the space between them.

"S'pose," Artemis said, placing her own hand on top of Poseidon's. "To Olympus, and beyond," she added, although for the life of her she didn't know why.

All at once electricity began to swathe them. There was a dull thrum and bits of litter circled them like hungry vultures. If you were to walk into that thin corridor between Marks and Spencer and Gregg's at that precise moment, if you were to see what was going on in there, it might very well have sent you mad. On the other hand, it might not, but nobody came and nobody saw, which was just as well.

Blue flashes bounced off the brickwork; out on the High Street, one of the G's fell from the Gregg's sign, but fortunately it made no difference in the grand scheme of things.

Artemis clenched her eyes tightly shut, for any moment now they would materialise in Pantheon, surrounded by irate gods and goddesses with questions on their lips, and Zeus would say, "What the bloody hell do you think you're playing at, young lady," to which she would reply, "I'm old enough to make my own decisions," and then Hera, as she so often did, would pipe up with, "You should listen to your father, Artemis," and she would reply with, "You're not my real mom!" which was the truth, because Wikipedia says so, and Wikipedia never lies.

She clenched her eyes, but when she opened them again they were not, as they thought they would be, back on Mount Olympus and in a whole heap of trouble.

They were in the same corridor of filth between Marks and Spencer and Gregg's. The blue electric was gone, and now, instead of it, there was a HTTP 404 ERROR NOT FOUND hanging there in thin air.

Poseidon looked shocked, which was about the right response. "I don't understand," he said.

"It means," said Artemis, "that the Wi-Fi's down."

"Impossible!"

"Not really," Artemis said, releasing Poseidon's hand. "It happens all the time here on Earth. In fact, people pay for the privilege. They like nothing more than to complain, you see, and with an Internet which only functions three times out of ten, and that's on a day when there's no electromagnetic storms, they get to complain a lot." She peeled a banana and began to eat it.

"That means we are stuck here," Poseidon said.

"Guess it does," Artemis replied, trying to sound disappointed about this unexpected turn of events[1].

"Bollocks!" said Poseidon.

"Now you're getting in the spirit!" Artemis said, pushing the rest of the banana into her face. "You're starting to fit in. Now, let's go and get Brahms and Liszt until such time as the portal to Olympus can be opened."

Poseidon did some frowning. He was, Artemis thought, very good at it. "Brahms and Liszt?" he said. "What is this Brahms and Liszt?"

"It means," Artemis said, "that we cross over the road, walk back the way we came, until we arrive at a quaint little establishment called 'The Fox'. When we get there, you go to the bar and order fifteen shots of whatever's on offer, while I nip to the Ladies."

A moment of silence passed between them, but before Artemis realised it was there Poseidon had started to speak again.

---

[1] As opposed to an expected turn of events, in which you know what's about to happen, and therefore it's not a turn of events at all. It's just an event.

"This 'The Fox' sounds very much like a pub," Poseidon said.

"Ah," said Artemis. "It does, doesn't it. But it's not just any old pub. It is something called a *Gastro*-pub."

Poseidon tried to wrap his mouth around the word. It was one of those words you always did a double-take of if you saw it written down. In the end, he decided to shake his head instead.

"No, me neither," Artemis said, walking toward the end of the passageway. Poseidon bounded after her.

Artemis silently thanked the God of Intolerable Wi-Fi Connectivity[1] as they went.

*

Ares rode on through the streets of Stepney, stopping only once to allow a small question-mark-shaped lady to cross the road. There was a joke in there somewhere, but Ares was not one for jokes.

That was Hermes' department.

And if Hermes had been present, he would have

---

[1] Sir Richard Branson has been called many things since founding Virgin all those years ago, but this was the first time he had been called a God. Needless to say, he rather liked it.

said, "Why did the small question-mark-shaped lady cross the road?" And Ares would have replied with a short, swift kick to Hermes' nethers, because there was nothing remotely funny about it.

"Freeze!" a voice called from somewhere behind Ares. When he turned, he saw that the voice belonged to a fat man in blue who appeared to be carrying an aubergine.

"I will smite thee!" Ares said, drawing his sword, to which the man responded by running in the opposite direction as fast as his legs could carry him.

Ares sheathed his sword and gave Shadow a firm kick to the ribs. "Yah!" he said.

As he went, the little old question-mark-shaped lady rudely gestured to him with two arthritic fingers.

18

Spinelli sighed into the phone. "How awful," he said. "And this cyclist just came out of nowhere, did it?" He had been on hold to the hospital for seven full minutes, even though *they* had called *him*. But now the nurse had returned to explain matters more fully.

"Yes, I'm afraid your friend is in rather a bad state at the moment," she said. "Heavy concussion, it would seem, coupled with a missing finger."

"Oh dear!" Spinelli said, feigning concern. "How unfortunate does one have to be to lose a finger to a speeding cyclist."

"Yes," said the nurse. "Fortunately, someone on scene must have bandaged it up. There's no sign of the finger in question, though. Or the poor man's larynx. We've had reports there's a bear out there, somewhere. In which case, the chances of finding the finger, or the larynx, are slim to none."

"By larynx," Spinelli said, "you mean..."

"His voice-box," said the nurse. "Yes, it's terrible, just terrible. I'm afraid your friend will never speak again."

"Oh, good," Spinelli said, for now he didn't have to concern himself with Vinnie talking to the cops. And then, "Um, I mean, oh good that it's not too serious." He sliced the end from a fat cigar and relaxed back in his chair. "Well, thanks for calling. I'm sure you have lots of things to be getting on with, so—"

"Actually, I'm trying to waste time," said the nurse. "It's my turn to clean out the toilets. I thought I might try to keep you on the line for as long as possible. Perhaps make it to around midday, so that I can sneak out for my lunch without first having to unblock a U-bend with nothing more protective than a pair of marigolds."

"Well, that sounds lovely," Spinelli said, "however, I'm a very busy man. Perhaps you should hide in a cupboard, or something."

"I've tried that," said the nurse. "But I'm awfully claustrophobic. It's a wonder I didn't go mad in the womb—"

"Yes, well, enjoy the rest of your day," Spinelli said, hanging up the phone.

No sooner had he hung up than terrible thoughts

began to run through his mind. Vinnie was out of the picture, written off by some arsehole in high-vis Lycra. Which meant that the Girl Guide, the old man with the big fork, and the prick with the expensive camera and propensity to hide in bushes were still out there. To top it all off, the chances of recouping the money Vinnie owed him were dropping by the second. All in all, it was a pretty bad day to be a London mobster.

A sudden, loud crash came from the other side of the door. This was quickly followed by grunts and groans, thumps and moans[1], and then a voice said, "You can't park that horse there!" Then something thumped into the door, and Spinelli leapt to his feet as slivers of wood flew through the air.

There was something stuck in the door, and now blood was dripping down from it.

"Bugger this!" Spinelli said, the cigar falling from his mouth. He raced across the office, pushed a painting aside[2], and began turning the dial of the safe

---

[1] Not the worst bit of poetry you'll ever hear, but it's right up there.

[2] You would think a man of Spinelli's stature would own a nice Hockney or Constable. He does not. The painting which

built into the wall. The combination was easy to remember; at least, it was if you weren't under immense pressure to get the damn thing open, in which case all notion of numbers, and stringing them together to reveal a memorable combination, were out the window.

Spinelli resorted to hitting the safe as hard as he could whilst at the same time shouting, in a very firm voice, "Let me have my guns, you selfish sock-sucker!" Needless to say, it did not work.

The door to his office slowly swung open. Spinelli turned, saw one of his men hanging there[1], pinned to the door by what appeared to be a golden spear, and said, "Whathafark?"

Allowing the painting to fall back over the safe, Spinelli backed away, pressing himself as hard as he could against the office wall and hoping that whoever was about to come through the door was simple of mind, and therefore might mistake him for a standing

conceals his safe is in fact a Tony Hart, worth somewhere in the region of eight-pound-fifty.
[1] The one who normally stands on the right.

lamp.

"Spinelli?" a jovial voice boomed. For a moment, Spinelli relaxed, for it was just his old friend Brian Blessed come for a chat.

However, the man who came through the door a moment later was not the aforementioned Blessed. He was some sort of hulking beast with a sword strapped to his waist and wearing what appeared to be a large red cape, which billowed around him as he moved, despite there not being a breath of air in the room.

"Jack Spinelli?" said the man as he removed his golden helmet and set it down on the desk. It looked incongruous there, next to Spinelli's favourite chocolate biscuits and his copy of *Mobstering for Dummies*.

Spinelli didn't answer. He was far too busy pretending to be a lamp.

"Come," said the man, settling into Spinelli's seat. "Take a seat. We have much to discuss, you and I, so the sooner you stop pretending to be a piece of furniture, the sooner we can get this show on the road."

"Who are you?" Spinelli said, falling out of

character for the first time. He wasn't cut out to be a standing lamp. In fact, he didn't know how they did it, standing there all day, not talking, only making a noise when someone pulled their cord. Remarkable, really, when you think about it.

The man sitting in Spinelli's big chair motioned to the small chair opposite. It was the chair Spinelli usually offered to the people he was about to remove fingers from, not least because it leaned a little to the left and made a strange squeaking noise whenever someone settled into it.

And now he was being ordered to sit in it by someone who wouldn't look out of place at a Greco-Persian war re-enactment. Had it not been the great big sword attached to the man's hip, Spinelli would have told him where he could go. As it was, he walked slowly and cautiously across the room and lowered himself into the small chair.

It squeaked beneath him, as he knew it would.

"You'll have to forgive me," the man said. "I'm not from around here."

"Ah," Spinelli said, fumbling about in his pocket for

a fresh cigar. It was a strange thing to be doing, for he didn't have a fresh cigar, or even a pocket, for that matter. "Northern, are you?"

"*Very* northern," the man said with a smile. Spinelli, who was not in on the joke, did not smile. "I'm actually from Ancient Greece."

"Oh," said Spinelli. "You mean back when they could afford things?"

"A little bit before then," said the man, who was, Spinelli noticed, growing increasingly frustrated. He motioned to Spinelli's bandaged hand, clicked his tongue, and said, "Nasty little wound you've got there."

Spinelli was slightly taken aback by the sudden change of subject. "It's healing," he said. "I'm sorry, I didn't catch your name."

"I didn't give it," said the man. "But since we are about to become partners, it seems only fair. My name is Ares, God of War, and I've recently moved here from Mount Olympus."

"You'll love the nightlife," Spinelli said. What he actually meant was, "The nightlife will love you," but he didn't have the balls to say so. "I think you've made some sort of huge mistake, sir," he went on. "This is reality. You appear to be living in some sort of fantasy-land. And, might I add, murder carries a very strict penalty in this fine country of ours, and since you've just murdered at least six of my men—" he turned and motioned to the one hanging from the door "—including whatsisname, you might want to consider hiring yourself a damn good lawyer. I have the number for one, if you want it. He's just got out of jail, so he'll be looking to rebuild his client list—"

"Did you notice," said the man, as calm as you like, "that throughout that little tirade of yours, your hand became unbearably itchy. So much so that, several times, you scratched at it like a madman?"

Spinelli had not noticed. But now that Ares had mentioned it, it was unbearably itchy.

"You might want to take a little look," said Ares, at which point he cracked his knuckles, lifted his legs, and plonked his size-twelve sandals down on the desk.

"Watch my biscuits!" Spinelli said. "I mean, um, please don't crush my biscuits." He quickly unwrapped the bandage from his hand, for it was itchier than ever now. "I… what…" Something was not right. And as he finally unravelled the bandage, he saw exactly what it was that was not right.

"Argh!" he cried, for there were maggots around the wound; hundreds of the little buggers. Not only around the wound, but somehow in it, popping in and out of the gaps between the stitches like some sort of post-mortem whack-a-mole. "I don't… get 'em out!"

The man, Ares, smiled and sighed at the same time. "Are you ready to talk business, Mr Spinelli?" he said, taking his feet from the desk, but leaving a few grains of sand behind.

"Yes! Yes! Just please! Help me!"

"Look at me," Ares said, and Spinelli looked at him, and for some reason the itchiness subsided almost immediately. "Now look at your hand."

Spinelli looked down to his hand. "How?" he said, with no small amount of incredulity, for there were no maggots there now. The wound was clean. As clean as a whistle[1], you might say, although whistles are, by definition, often unclean and filled with spittle. But there was no spittle in Spinelli's wound, and no sign of maggots, for which he was eternally grateful. "I don't understand."

"That is because you are mortal," Ares said, leaning in close. "And mortals do not understand magic, or gods, or the magic of gods. Now, Mr Spinelli, how would you like to change all that?"

Brushing sand from his beautiful desk, lest it scratch the mahogany, he said, "I'm not sure what you're proposing here," because he wasn't, "and I don't know whether what just happened really happened," which he didn't, "but I would love for you to elucidate."

"I'm sure you would," said Ares, "but I am a very shy man wearing very little as it is, and so instead I will explain the deal I am offering to you. I will make you, and your men, immortal. You will gather an army, and you will serve me until such time as I see fit to release

---

[1] The term actually refers to the pure, clean sound a whistle makes and was seemingly coined by a deaf man when it was still cool to make stuff up.

you from your duty. Together we will bring humanity to its knees. We will make slaves of them. They will fear us, and they will worship us."

"Sounds nice," Spinelli said once Ares paused long enough for him to slip a word in edgeways, "and I'd be lying if I said I wasn't intrigued, but didn't you already kill all my men? Isn't it a bit late to make them immortal?"

"It's never too late," said Ares, and with a flick of the wrist, the man pinned to the door by a golden spear began thrashing around. His movements were jerky, but they were movements nonetheless.

Spinelli watched in horror as his henchman reached down and began fingering the spear, seemingly confused as to what it was doing there and trying to figure out a way to stop it from being there. It was one of the most grotesque things Spinelli had ever seen, and yet he found it utterly mesmerising.

When he turned back, Ares was looking at him. More specifically he was looking at the wounded hand. "You seek vengeance," he said, "against the people responsible for that."

"Well, yes," Spinelli said. "I sent a man to track them down, but he's in hospital now with a missing larynx."

Ares laughed. "Doesn't surprise me," he said. "You cannot send a mortal to fight a god. It will almost always end in the hospitalisation, or mortuary-isation, of the mortal."

"Actually," Spinelli said, finally locating a half-smoked cigar and popping it between his lips, "my man was run down by a cyclist."

"A cyclist?"

"Yes, it's sort of, well, it's a man on two wheels."

"Ah!" Ares said. "I think I know what you're talking about. Those arseholes that wear skin-tight yellow suits?"

"That's the one," Spinelli said, flicking his lighter and then chasing the flame with the cigar.

"Would you like me to help your man?" Ares said. "The one in hospital?"

Spinelli gave it some serious thought. What Ares was suggesting, what he was offering to do, was make Vinnie 'The Jockstrap' Aiello immortal. Strength in numbers, and all that. After an indeterminate amount of time, Spinelli said, "Nah." And that was about the gist of it.

"In that case," Ares said, "let us set our plan in motion." He stood, walked around the desk, and placed hands upon Spinelli's shoulders. He was, Spinelli noticed, extremely strong, but that's the thing with Greek gods. "You are now immortal, Mr Spinelli with powers beyond your wildest imagination."

"Really?" Spinelli said, reaching for a biscuit. "Because I don't feel any different." The biscuit crumbled in his hand. "Oh!" he said. "That's never happened before." And he hoped it would never happen again, for he really fancied a biscuit and if they were going to crumble every time he picked one up, well, he'd have to get quicker at transferring them from plate to mouth.

"Perhaps not the best demonstration of your new strength," Ares said. "Try it on something else."

"Such as?" Spinelli glanced around the office.

"I don't know," said Ares. "Do you have, perhaps, a very big book. One with lots of pages that you could not possibly tear down the middle?"

"Of course!" Spinelli said, and he stood and walked across the room to where, upon a filing cabinet, sat this year's edition of the telephone directory. Year upon year the directory grew thicker. The 2017 edition was almost as thick as *War and Peace*, and only slightly less boring if you were to read it in from Aaronovitch to Zyskowski[1]. He gripped the directory tightly and was suddenly aware of a strange feeling deep within him. It was a feeling that said he could bloody well do this and, eager to prove it, he proceeded to rip the directory clean in half. When all around him lay the pages of the book, he said, "Fricking hell!"

Ares, who was now helping him to half a pint of scotch, applauded. "See!" he said. "Now imagine what you could do to a mortal."

Spinelli imagined it, all the while staring down at his impossibly strong hands. "It's real," he said. "You're real."

"Of course I'm real," Ares said, dropping a

---

[1] Having done this purely for research purposes, I can assure you it picks up around Dungworth, and if you stick with it, there's a plot twist you'll never see coming around the E.L. Shufflebottom mark.

miniature umbrella into his drink.

"Will somebody get me down from here, please?" said the man pinned to the door.

"In a minute, whatsisname," Spinelli said. To Ares he said, "This army you want me to summon? Can it be anyone?"

Ares smiled, and it was a terribly evil smile, the way a shark might smile when presented with a surfing tournament. "Anyone," he said.

Spinelli nodded. "Let me make a few calls," he said. "I know a few good men."

"I'm a good man," said the one on the door. "If you'd just get me down."

"Can you," Spinelli said to Ares, "undo the immortality thingy."

"I can indeed," Ares replied, dipping a biscuit in his scotch. Spinelli, out of the corner of his mouth—which is the right way to do it if you don't want anyone to know what you're saying—instructed Ares to put the man hanging on the door out of his misery. "Oh!" Ares said. "Yeah, no worries." And with a flick of the wrist the man on the door fell limp again. "You're a cruel,

cruel man," Ares said. "I think we're going to get along just fine."

"I have a few calls to make," Spinelli said. "Help yourself to a biscuit."

He picked up the phone and began to dial.

19

The Fox was, like most London pubs, filled to the extent it was almost impossible to move. If you wanted something from the bar, it was best to tell the person wedged in front of you and ask them if they would be so kind as to pass it along. Alternatively, you could stand on a table and yell your order in the general direction of the barman, who would in turn inform you that you should pass your order on to the person wedged in front, the way everyone else does.

Fortunately, such rules did not apply to the God of the Sea and the Goddess of the Hunt, who, upon entering the establishment, parted the crowd as if they were the Red Sea. Some of them complained about it, but when they realised their complaints were falling upon deaf ears they got on with whatever it was they had been doing a moment ago, i.e. passing their order to the person in front and hoping that by the time it reached the barman, it wasn't something silly like, "Two pints of giblets and a packet of shoes."

"This is ridiculous," Poseidon said, fending off drunkards with his trident.

Artemis was not listening. She was too busy trying to attract the attention of the barman, who appeared to be busying himself with the daily crossword at the end of the bar. However, he lost all interest in the answer to twenty-one down[1] when an arrow whipped past his face, causing his hair to go all aflutter, before burying itself in the treble-twenty of the dartboard on the other side of the pub.

"What can I get you?" said the barman, somewhat reluctantly. Artemis couldn't help but notice the strange way in which his eyes went off in different directions. Poseidon took up a stool at the bar next to Artemis.

"You must be related to Costas," Poseidon said.

"Who?" replied the bartender in a manner which suggested he was considering calling last orders and to hell with the lost profits.

"Same..." Poseidon motioned to his own eyes. "Anyway, enough of this nonsense. Fifteen shots of whatever's on offer while my friend here goes to the

---

[1] The answer was forty-two, which seemed to be the general consensus no matter who you asked.

Ladies."

"There's nothing on offer," the barman said. "This is London. Not some fairy-tale."

"We'll have two pints then, if you please," Artemis said.

"Two pints each?" said the barman.

"One pint each," Poseidon said as he drummed his finger upon the sticky bar, "thusly adding up to two pints in total."

"Why didn't you stand at the back of the room and pass your order to the person in front?" the barman asked as he set about pouring two pints of unnameable. "That's how we do things here in London, which means you're not from around here, which means I'm going to have to ask you for I.D." He placed the pints down on the bar but kept his filthy little hands wrapped around them. "Also, I'm having trouble believing you're older than twelve. It's the Girl Guide uniform, you see. Dead giveaway."

"I.D.?" Artemis said, in that way people do when they haven't a clue what's being asked of them.

"Identification," said the barman. "Usually a bit of

card with a picture of your face on it."

How absurd, Artemis thought. Where would you even get something like that? A bit of card with a picture of your face on it? What a strange world the humans had created for themselves.

"Well," Poseidon said, "we do not possess such a thing, however I can assure you that I am who I say I am, and this here is Artemis, and she too is who I say she is, and she is old enough to drink, so can we have our drinks now, please?"

The barman seemed flummoxed. "Um," he said. "I s'pose so." And he pushed the pints toward them. "That'll be eighteen-pound-fifty, please."

Artemis looked at Poseidon and Poseidon looked off into the middle-distance. After almost a minute of this, she turned to the barman and said, "We're actually meeting someone here. Someone with at least eighteen-pound-fifty in his pocket. In fact, I have it on good authority that he'll be carrying twice that, so how about another two pints?"

The barman's eyes flitted this way and that as he tried to make sense of what he was being told. In the end, he decided to go with his gut instinct, and that was to pour another two pints and collect the money when their associate arrived. Later, he would regret the decision. He would, in fact, lose sleep over it. It would drive him so crazy that, for at least an hour, his eyes straightened. But that was later on, and this was now, and that was that.

With their pints in hand, Artemis and Poseidon pushed through the crowd, eyes peeled for a free table.

"Is anyone sitting here?" Artemis asked as they arrived at a table that wasn't free.

"Yes," said one of the men sitting there. "*We* are."

Artemis looked at the man, and she looked at the man, and after several uncomfortable moments he decided it wasn't worth the hassle and got to his feet. His friends, of which there were two, did the same. They skulked off toward the pool table, set a coin down on it, and waited for the game presently taking place to reach a suitable conclusion, which, more often than not, was the moment one of the players got clobbered around the head with a pool cue.

Once seated, Artemis said, "This is the life, hey?"

"It is *a* life," Poseidon said, supping at his beer.

"I could really get used to it," Artemis said, taking a long draft of her own. It was warm, and there was a slight aftertaste of cabbage that she wasn't sure was meant to be there, but it was refreshing nonetheless. "Fancy a game of pool?"

"I most certainly do not," Poseidon said, glancing across to the pool table in time to see one of the players get clobbered about the head with a pool cue. A further scuffle broke out as a piece of the broken pool cue landed in an innocent bystander's pint. It was all very messy. "Look at them. Animals, they are. The sooner we get out of here, the better. And what was all that about meeting someone? Once the barman realises we've made a dunce of him, we're for it."

Artemis sniggered. "You're not afraid of a wonky-eyed barman from Stepney, are you?" She sniggered again; Poseidon looked at her as if he wished he had a pool cue. "Oh, come on," she said. "Lighten up. Think of this as an adventure. We're a couple of adventurers from another realm, and this—" she motioned to their surroundings "—this is our Mordor."

"That would explain the orcs over by the fruit machine and the hobbits being turfed out by the door supervisors." He took out his π∑∏ and began prodding at the keys.

"Who are you calling?" Artemis asked as she fished some kind of six-legged black thing from her beer.

"Zeus," Poseidon said, pressing the π∑∏ to his ear. "We have to tell him that we tried to get back, but technology prevented us from doing so."

"Technology," Artemis said, pointing to the π∑∏, "is also stopping you from getting laid."

Poseidon shushed her, which was rather rude, Artemis thought. She didn't like being shushed. It was, she thought, far quicker and less impolite to simply say, "Quiet." Still, Poseidon was het up, so she let it slide on this occasion. Next time, he'd get a bunch of arrows to the sternum.

"It's just ringing," Poseidon said.

Artemis glanced about the thin air all around them. "They could be watching us right now," she said. And with that, she stuck her middle finger in the air, just in case.

Poseidon hung up and placed the $\pi\sum\prod$ down on the table. It was a wonky table, and the $\pi\sum\prod$'s weight caused it to rock. "Something's not right," he said, frowning. "Zeus always picks up."

"I wouldn't worry about it," Artemis said. That was the thing about gods being immortal; you never had to concern yourself with the wellbeing of family members. If you were woken in the middle of the night by a frantic rapping upon the door, and if you answered said door to find an Ephor standing there looking as if he'd just lost the Shield of Ajax and found a drachma, you could take solace in the fact that no one was dead.

Never the less, Poseidon appeared to be worrying about it.

"Look, we'll finish these," she said, motioning to their drinks, "and then we'll try to get back again. I'm sure it's just a dodgy connection."

"You're right," Poseidon said. "I'm just being silly."

"Yes." Artemis lifted her drink and held it forward. "Cheers."

"What?"

"Never mind."

20

The office was thick with cigarette smoke, which was just how Simian liked it, and there didn't appear to be a rat within six-feet of him, despite the fact that they were known for such things. It was, according to the clock hanging above the door, a little after midday, but then the clock hanging over the door always said that. Simian kept forgetting to put a new battery in it.

A blank sheet of paper sat on the desk in front of him. Well, it wasn't entirely blank; Simian had doodled a rather distorted man's appendage in one corner of it. But apart from that it was completely blank.

He quickly, and in illegible cursive, scribbled two words across the page, and those words were Margot and Trix. Spelling was not his strongest point, and so what he'd actually written was Margow Tricks, but he knew what he meant, and that was all that mattered.

After doodling a second, equally anatomically incorrect penis in the opposite corner of the page, he sat back in his seat and sighed.

So she was an undercover cop and a redhead at the same time. That was a deadly combination. It was a wonder she hadn't shot herself in the face by now. "Perhaps red is not her natural colour," he said to the cockroach scuttling off across the office carpet. It stopped for a moment before continuing its journey. Simian made a mental note to call the exterminator[1]. And then the carpet shop to find out when they were going to deliver his new Arabian red drugget.

For reasons unknown, he glanced at the clock again.

Stella Spinelli should have arrived by now, but Simian hoped she had forgotten about their plan to meet. He had nothing to give her. Well, that wasn't entirely true. He had photos of her husband placing his head inside a redhead's mouth in front of Harry Ramsden's, but he couldn't give her those, not now he knew the redhead was an undercover cop. It had all gone, as they say in the trade, a bit tits-up. The only thing worse than not being able to give Stella the photographs was having to give her back the cheque she had so generously handed to him just yesterday.

---

[1] Although it would have made more sense to call a presently-employed terminator.

He could have used that money to put toward an exterminator, or a battery for the clock hanging over the door.

The door which was now being gently knocked by a silhouette.

"Come in," Simian said as he quickly folded up the sheet of paper with two dicks and a misspelled name on it and hid it away in his desk drawer. "I said come—"

"I'm already in," Stella said. And she was. Not only was she in, but she was already sitting in the chair opposite, looking all sultry. It was, Simian thought, the look a female praying mantis gives to its partner when it's feeling a little horny. To which the male praying mantis usually replies, "Not tonight, love. Got a bit of a headache." At least, it does if it's got any sense.

Simian eased the desk drawer shut. "Ah," he said. "You didn't happen to see what I just did there, did you?"

"Mr Knight!" she said. "If you are for one minute suggesting that I saw you fold that piece of paper, upon which you had drawn two elephants and some sort of heavy-metal band logo, then I am shocked, Mr Knight! Shocked and appalled!"

"I'm sorry," Simian said. "Can't be too careful."

Stella lit a cigarette and added to the fug already dancing around the office like lost clouds. "I take it you have what I came for?"

Lie to her, Simian thought. Lie to her, tell her your camera broke, and that everything that was on it was erased.

"My camera broke," he said. "Everything that was on it was era—"

"This camera?" Stella said, for she had somehow found Simian's safe and plumbed in the correct combination. Either that or Simian had forgotten to put the camera in the safe, as he had planned to, and she had simply picked it up from the desk, which now that Simian thought about it was a more likely scenario.

"There is absolutely nothing on there," Simian said, reaching across the desk in an attempt to relieve her of the camera. But despite his name, he had regular-sized arms, and so came away empty-handed.

"There appears to be quite a bit on here," Stella said as she watched and flicked through the images on the viewfinder. "Lots of pictures of you hiding in bushes, it seems."

"When it's dark," Simian said, "it's hard to know which way the camera is pointing."

Stella suddenly became very concerned. Simian could tell she was concerned by the way her eyelashes fluttered. He knew she had reached the pictures of her husband doing the dirty with the redhead. His number was up, so to speak, and so was Simian's.

"Is this some kind of terrible joke?" Stella said, her finger hitting the NEXT button on the camera so fast that Simian could no longer see it. The smoke didn't help.

"I'm afraid not, Mrs Spinelli," Simian said. He had no choice but to give her the pictures now. "For an extra tenner I do a lovely package. You get a snow-globe, two keyrings, and a 3D hologram engraved in a block of glass—"

"No, Mr Knight," said Stella, "these photographs are all of you hiding in a bush. There is one of what appears to be a millipede going, 'Rargh', but other than that they are of no use to me."

"Really?" Simian said, hoping she didn't sense his joy. "Well, that's a turn up for the books. I never saw that coming. What an awful shame. I guess I have absolutely no proof that your husband is doing the dirty on you with the redhead from the chippie."

Stella was fuming, Simian could tell she was fuming by the way her eyes were twitching. The smoke didn't help. "You are useless, Mr Knight," she said. "An utter disgrace to your profession."

Simian couldn't argue with her there, so he didn't. "You know, you're not the first person to say that," he said as he slid open his desk drawer and riffled about until he located the cheque. "You'll be wanting this back, I presume?"

She snatched the proffered cheque out of his hand and stood. Simian could tell she was standing by the way she was on her legs. "I will have no choice but to take my business elsewhere."

"In that case," Simian said, "I will have no choice but to accept your decision and wish you all the best."

She huffed, turned, and marched toward the door, muttering something about incompetence as she went.

Simian couldn't believe his luck. He had, by way of complete ineptitude, avoided getting caught up in an undercover investigation. Once he was certain Stella had left the building, he jumped for joy and whooped and hollered.

Downstairs, ten more old folks dropped dead, but he wasn't to know that.

He threw on his trench-coat, balanced his jaunty little fedora atop his head, and headed down to his local to celebrate.

21

It is not unusual to find a white van parked outside one's building. A toilet gets blocked, you place a call and a man arrives in a white van. A pigeon gets stuck in the ventilation ducts running all through the building, a man armed with a net and a copy of 'Pigeons and How to Handle Them Without Losing an Eye' arrives in a white van. White vans are the choice of vehicle for tradesmen across the land. If a man in a red van were to show up, you would send it and the man away. Everyone knows that.

But the white van currently parked in front of SPINELLI'S had been sitting there for weeks. No one had ordered it, and no one had noticed it, because it was a white van. Even a camouflaged van would have stuck out more than this one.

Inside the van, two suited men sat in front of banks of monitors, sweating and cursing, stopping occasionally to help themselves to a doughnut. It was your classic stakeout, right down to the fine details. On the plethora of screens lining both sides of the interior, live feeds from Jack Spinelli's club played out in real time, which was how live feeds often worked. There was, in fact, a one-second delay, which apparently a second white van had been ordered to put right, but it was yet to arrive, and so the two suited men (let's call them agents, for that is indeed what they were) watched the screens and ate doughnuts and, when things were a little quiet, turned their attention to another screen at the front of the van which played M*A*S*H reruns.

The agents were bored. One of them even said so, to which the other replied, "Why don't we watch the M*A*S*H monitor for a bit. Nothing seems to be happening in the club. What difference is it going to make if we turn our backs on the monitors for an hour or so? I'm sure nothing is going to happen while we're not looking."

An hour passed, in which Radar was awarded a hardship discharge and, as a result, B.J. and Klinger got hopelessly drunk. It was a pleasant way to spend an hour, and would have been even more pleasant had they not run out of doughnuts by the second episode.

"Maybe we ought to get back to work," said Agent

One[1]. "DePayne will have our guts for garters if we miss something."

"You're not afraid of a little redhead, are you?" said Agent Two[2].

"Hey, she's as tough as she is red," said Agent One. "I once saw her take down a cage-fighter using just one hand." It was true, although what he forgot to mention that the hand in question had a hammer in it. "Trust me, you do not want to get on the wrong side of—"

The doors at the back of the van suddenly flew open. "The wrong side of who?" said Kelly DePayne, a.k.a. Margot Trix. She climbed into the back of the van, pulling the doors shut behind her. The smell of fish and battered sausage suddenly permeated the air, and would continue to do so until a man in a white van came along six months later to hose it down.

"Um," said Agent Two. "Joseph Merrick."

"Joseph Merrick?" DePayne asked.

---

[1] His real surname is Orange, but for obvious reasons he refuses to go by it.

[2] Which *is* his real surname. His first name is Juan, which is a strange name for a born-and-bred cockney, proving what a pair of jokers his parents are.

"Yeah, you don't want to get on the wrong side of Joseph Merrick," Agent One said. "Not before breakfast, at least."

DePayne looked at him as if he'd just pissed on her foot. "Turn M*A*S*H off," she said. "I need a full report. Everything that's been said in the past twelve hours, every move Spinelli's made, transcriptions of every phone call he's received, I want it all and I want it an hour ago."

She sat down on one of the swivel chairs and glanced up at the bank of monitors in front of her.

She said, "What the fuck?" which was about the correct response for what she was seeing on the multiple screens.

Agent One leaned it, and when he saw what she was looking at, he said, "Bloody hell!"

"Don't tell me Spinelli's naked again," said Agent Two, and then he, too, saw what they were looking at, and added, "Jesus H. Christmas!"

There had, if the monitors were to be believed—and there was no reason *not* to believe them as they cost a pretty penny—been some kind of a massacre.

There were bodies everywhere, and where there wasn't a body there was a puddle of black blood, for the monitors might have cost a pretty penny, but apparently did not come with colour as standard.

"Get everyone down here right now," DePayne said. "We need to get in there, find out if one of those bodies is Spinelli." She stood, made her way to the doors at the back of the van. "You two are in deep shit for this," she said across her shoulder, before throwing open the doors and jumping down onto the road.

It was difficult, Agent One thought, to take threats seriously from a woman with pickled cockles in her ears, but she was fuming. Agent One knew she was fuming because the cockle in her ear had been slowly cooking.

"This is all your fault," said Agent One.

"No it's not," replied Agent Two. "It's yours."

After three whole minutes of back and forth, they arrived at the conclusion they were both to blame, and that the best course of action was damage limitation.

Agent One called the Met while Agent Two placed an order for more doughnuts.

22

Mount Olympus had been sitting there, minding its own business, since the dawn of time. You really couldn't miss it, for it a was big bastard of a mountain and therefore unmissable. But now that it was missing, the locals had begun to notice. And, as so often happens when a huge outcrop decides to vanish into thin air, panic ensued.

"It was there a minute ago," said one bystander.

"It is the Devil's work," said another, which was not far from the truth.

"I'm sure if we wait patiently," said a third, "it'll turn up. Have any of you looked down the cushions of your sofas?"

*

Zeus paced back and forth across the meeting room. It was the mindless wandering of a god on the edge, which was fortunate as that was what he was. He punched a number into his $\pi\sum\prod$ for the umpteenth time and waited.

"He's not going to answer, dear," Hera said. She had

calmed down a little, now that her initial shock had subsided.

"He bloody well better," Zeus said. Sparks flew from the tip of his thunderbolt. "This is ridiculous. I've seen some ridiculous things in my time, but—" his sentence was cut abruptly off by a deep grunt from the π∑∏'s speaker. "Hades? Is that you? You'd better speak up, brother, or so help me—"

"Zeus," said Hades. "Now's not a good time. I'm just off to Elysium to get a carton of milk."

"Don't be so bloody daft," Zeus said. He knew Hades didn't take milk in his coffee. "You've got a lot of explaining to do."

There was a second of silence. Zeus could practically hear the cogs going around in his brother's head. "Is this about the void thing?"

"Of *course* it's about the void thing!" Zeus said, before turning to Hera and throwing his arms wide as if to say, *What else could it be about?* "You need to put this mountain back where it belongs. People are going to start to notice it's not there, and frankly I'm sick of looking out the window and seeing nothing for miles in all directions."

"I told Ares I didn't want to do it," Hades said. "I said, 'This is going to piss your father off, so I'm not going to be a part of it'. But he can be extremely persuasive, can Ares."

"I don't care if he held a sword to your throat and a dagger to your nethers. You're fiddling in business that doesn't concern you."

"I said that," Hades explained. "I told him that whatever it was he wanted to get back at you for, it had nothing to do with me, but like I said, he can be very persuasive."

Zeus sighed. "What did he offer you?" He walked across to the table and picked up an abacus. "Whatever it is, I'll double it. Just put us back where we belong and we'll speak no more of it." Zeus kept his fingers crossed as he made the offer, for this was not something he could just brush under the carpet and forget it ever happened. There would be consequences; there had to be consequences, otherwise everyone would think he had gone soft, and a soft god is about as useful as a screen door on a submarine.

"Well, he offered to walk Cerberus for me twice a day," Hades finally said.

"I can do that!" Zeus said. "Twice a day? Heck, I'll do it thrice a day!"

"It's not as easy as it sounds," Hades said. "Those little poo bags simply don't cut it. You have to carry a shovel and a hessian sack with you."

"Not a problem," Zeus said. "How is he with other dogs?"

"They get stuck in his teeth," Hades said.

"Oh," Zeus said. "Well, I'll just have to keep him on a leash."

Hades sighed. A waft of warm air seeped from the $\pi\sum\prod$, and Zeus had to take his face away momentarily, lest he find himself missing a few layers of skin. "Okay, but you have to know, I had no choice in this. Ares held a sword to my throat and a dagger to my nethers."

"All is forgiven," Zeus said. It surprised him how easy it was to lie to his brother. "Now, be a sport and—"

The room began to shake. Paintings fell from the wall, and in rooms all around the palace unwary gods cried out, for it must have come as quite a shock. Zeus staggered this way and that, like William Shatner trying to latch onto Spock, a sexy green alien, anything to prevent himself from falling over.

This went on for a few moments, and as it did, Hades hummed a tuneless ditty down the line, as if he were performing nothing more taxing than removing a tick. When in fact a lot of work went into throwing an entire mountain about the place. You had to be careful, for you were never more than one thought away from dropping it on the moon.

"All done!" Hades said after what seemed like an eternity. "Now, Cerberus likes to go out early in the mornings, as that's when he does his big poo—"

Zeus hung up, rushed across to the window, and looked down and out[1]. He saw the heavens and the earth, saw the light and that it was good, saw the crowd of confused Greeks gathered at the bottom of the mountain, and decided to get the hell away from

---

[1] As in the direction of his gaze, and not that he was suddenly wearing shoes with holes in them and a trench-coat that suggested he was quite possibly naked underneath.

the window before they started blaming him.

"Put the kettle on, love," Zeus said.

To Earth he would go, and woe betide Ares for what he had done.

But not before a nice cup of tea and a packet of chocolate biscuits.

23

"I said," Simian yelled into the face of the person in front, "tell Colin I want a pint of scotch, a packet of dry-roasted peanuts, and the key to the disabled toilet." The person in front, who Simian had only just noticed was wearing a hearing-aid, turned around and began to convey the message forward. Simian held little hope that his order would be correct by the time it arrived at Colin. There was a very good chance he would be leaving The Fox with a packet of AA batteries, two pantomime dwarves, and an annual subscription to Farmer's Fortnightly.

Order placed, Simian glanced about the bar, hoping to alight upon someone with him he was acquainted. The events of the last twenty-four hours or so had made him realise just how much he missed the mundane. It was nice to not be shot with golden arrows. It was nice to not wake up in the middle of the night to discover a woman swathed in gold looming over you like some sort of blazing angel. It was nice to not have to worry about whether he was encroaching upon a major criminal investigation, although it was not nice to have a cheque cruelly snatched away from him before he'd even had a chance for it to bounce.

There was no one in the bar that he recognised, mainly because he could only see the backs of the head of the five people crammed in tight all around him.

"Here you go, mate," said the deaf bloke, and thrust a Crème de menthe in his general direction.

"I..." Simian began, before quickly deciding it wasn't worth the hassle and taking the drink without further fuss.

He slipped through the throng of drunken humanoids as easily as a fat person might traverse a swimming pool. By the time he emerged somewhere next to the fruit machine, which appeared to be on the blink again, he was barren of breath and had split half his green drink.

Still, it was his own fault. He should have anticipated such a crowd on a Tuesday lunchtime.

"I'll play the winner," he said, placing a fifty-pence piece down on the edge of the pool table.

"We broke all the cues," said a man with a black eye. "We're just using our arms now."

Simian picked up his coin and sighed. Still, it was nice to get back to normality.

He walked across the sticky floor, which took a lot longer than it should have, and arrived at the dartboard. It was then that he noticed the golden arrow sticking out of the treble twenty, and his bowels decided that now was as good a time as any to loosen somewhat.

"No," he said. "I'm not seeing it. It's not real."

An elderly gent with a patch covering his right eye must have overheard, for he came across to where Simian stood, paralysed, and said, "We've tried yanking it out, but it's not budging."

"Wha—"

"The golden arrow," the man said, pointing at it with a finger he didn't have[1]. "Reckon Colin needs to order a new board."

"Yes," Simian said, sipping upon his Crème de menthe and wishing it was something else. "The

---

[1] For he had defaulted on a fifty pound loan he had taken out with Spinelli, but that's another story entirely and in no way advances the plot of this particular one.

person responsible," he said, "did you happen to get a good look at them?"

The man nodded. "Oh, yes!" he said. "I might be missing an eye, but I know a twelve-year-old Girl Guide when I see one."

"Gah!" Simian said, which was a noise had hadn't made in at least a couple of hours.

"What's the matter?" asked the man. "You look like you've seen a ghost, or perhaps something a little less cliché."

"This... Girl Guide?" Simian said, giving up on the green drink and offering it to a fella on the way to the toilet.

"Piss off," said the fella, which is about the correct response when someone offer you a half-finished glass of Crème de menthe.

Simian set his glass down on the edge of the bar and said, "You saw her... I mean, she was here, and you saw her fire that arrow into the dartboard?"

"It is," said the man, "impossible to fire an arrow. I believe they use the term 'shoot', you see. Best to get the vernacular right, that's what I say."

Simian resisted the urge to punch the old man on the nose. "Yes, quite, but she was here, yes? And you saw her with your very eye?"

"That I did," said the old man. "In fact, I think she's still here somewhere." He turned and began scouring the pub, though not in the literal sense, although it could have done with a good scouring. As well as fumigating, burning, and rebuilding from the foundations up. "There she is," the man said. "Sitting on that table over there with that old bloke." He turned to Simian, who had frozen once again. "Can you believe, in this day and age, people still leave the house wearing sandals? Shocking, isn't it. Anyway, must dash. The missus'll be wondering where I've got to." And the old man dashed, leaving Simian there with his mouth all agape and without a drink in his hand.

This is, Simian thought, entirely crazy, but he thought it as his legs carried him toward the table around which sat the Girl Guide and the old man with the big fork. Of the golden witch who had singed a hole in his office carpet, there was no sign. Perhaps she was off, causing damage to other people's floor coverings.

"You're real," Simian said to both the man and girl. They looked up at him as if they should recognise him, perhaps had met him at some point, yet couldn't quite put their finger on it. Simian didn't know what was worse: that these arseholes were here in his local, or that they shot so many people with arrows that they didn't recognise one of their victims when he walks right up to them and says, "You're real."

"Oh!" the girl said, suddenly more animated than a chunk of Nick Park's plasticine. "You're the... I almost didn't recognise you without drool on your face."

The old man shrugged. "Nope," he said. "Not a clue."

Before Simian had a chance to remind the old fart about the events of the previous night, the girl piped up again. "He's the pervert with the camera!" she said, entirely too loudly for Simian's liking.

Silence. The Fox's patrons turned, their faces all a-frown as they tried to decide whether there was about to be a fight, and then wondering whether they had time to get involved before nipping off home for a few hours' kip before stumbling back for the evening session. It turned out that it just wasn't worth the trouble, and the volume went back up again.

"I'm not a pervert," Simian said. "I'm a private investigator, and last night I was investigating privately when you—" he jabbed an accusatory finger at the girl "—decided to put an arrow into my shoulder."

The girl sipped on her beer as if butter wouldn't melt. "If it's any consolation," she said, "I was aiming for your face."

"Take a seat, Mr Knight," said the old man, and he pushed an empty chair out from under the table with his foot.

Simian sat, his heart pounding so quickly in his chest that he thought, for a moment, that Colin had started the Tuesday night disco early. "How do you know my name?" he asked.

"The same way we found your address last night," the old man said. "We went through your wallet."

Something suddenly occurred to Simian, something to do with an expired condom, but he quickly dismissed it as not at all worth worrying about. "I don't remember much about last night," he said.

"Other than the agonising pain, of course, and the woman swathed in gold who loomed over me and burned a hole in my carpet."

There passed, between the old man and the girl, a look. "We shouldn't," said the old man.

"But look at him," said the girl. Simian found it rather odd that she was halfway down what appeared to be her second pint. "If we don't tell him, it'll drive him crazy, and I don't think I could live with myself if he ended up in the loony bin."

"Telling him might send him there, too," said the old man.

"Tell me what?" Simian said, for the suspense was killing him. It was like watching an episode of *Murder She Wrote*, only a lot less tedious. He was suddenly very aware that he did not have a drink.

"Okay," the girl said. "But you have to keep it to yourself. We're going home in a bit, and the last thing we need is some private investigator shouting his mouth off to all and sundry."

"I'm very discreet," Simian said, intrigued. He leaned in, for he imagined they would all be talking out of the sides of their mouths for the next couple of minutes.

"We're gods," said the girl. Just like that, as if she were telling him nothing more important than what had happened in last night's Game of Thrones. She then went on to tell him how they came to be in Stepney, why she looked like a twelve-year-old Girl Guide when in fact she was older than most Chinese vases. By the time she got around to the strange gadget sitting on the table in front of Poseidon (Poseidon! As in the guy from Percy Jackson!) Simian had started to struggle.

"And Zeus is your father," Simian said, not quite a question. "And he's angry with you because you shouldn't be here amongst us mortals."

"Angry might be putting it mildly," Poseidon said. "I should imagine he's already picturing where he's going to shove his thunderbolt when we return."

Simian had spent much of the past twenty-four hours with his mouth agape, and now was no different. A fly, which had been hovering around Artemis' beer, decided to pop in and see if there was anything worth pilfering. It flew out a second later, no doubt disappointed and slightly damper than it had been a moment ago.

"You'll have to forgive me," Simian said, finally. "This is a lot to take in."

The girl, Artemis, shrugged. "Take it or leave it. It makes no difference to us."

"I read about you guys in History," Simian said.

"Some of it's probably true," Poseidon said.

"Didn't you have a run-in with Odysseus?" It had been a while since Simian left school, and at the time he never thought he'd have a use for all the toff they thrust upon him, but here he was, sitting at a table with a couple of Greek gods. Maybe next week he'd meet Pythagoras in the supermarket queue.

Poseidon winced at the mention of his adversary's name. "Let's just say Odysseus was a bit of a git and leave it at that."

Simian nodded. "Sure," he said, for the great big fork leaning against the table looked capable of inflicting serious damage. "And the woman swathed in gold? Is she a goddess, too?"

Poseidon rubbed at his neck as if he had a crick in it. "Aceso," he said. "She's the Goddess of Curing Sickness and Healing Wounds."

"And also Burning Carpets," Simian said.

"That was," Poseidon said, "unfortunate. Think of it like this: if she hadn't turned up when she did, you would have bled out. A holey carpet is a small price to pay for being brought back from the brink of death."

"It was a very nice carpet," Simian said, though he wasn't sure why.

Artemis yawned and fished yet another fly from her beer. "So, what's the deal with you and the man trying to devour the redhead?" She flicked the fly across the room, where it landed on the back of a bald man's head. He didn't seem to notice.

"Spinelli?" Simian said. "I was paid to obtain proof he was running around behind his wife's back with the dame from the chip shop. That's what I was in the middle of doing when you shot me. I provide a service, you see. Think your spouse is cheating? Come to me. Lost your cat? Come to me. Need to track down a long-lost relative? Go to someone else. My forte is really cheaters and cats." He lit a cigarette, remembered that The Fox had finally succumbed to the smoking ban, and crushed it out on the edge of the wonky table. "This job, the Spinelli job, had a twist even I didn't see coming, and I'm not talking about the interference of a couple of ancient deities, either." He took out a vaping pipe and began to suck on it. "Turns out the redhead is an undercover cop. They've been investigating Spinelli for some time. Trafficking, drugs, embezzlement, he's done it all, and he's got the copy of *Mobstering for Dummies* to prove it.

"I think I dodged a bullet, if I'm being completely honest."

"But not an arrow," Artemis said, not without humour.

"Yes, quite," Simian said.

Colin the barman materialised from the crowd. "You," he said to Simian, "must be the guy who's got at least thirty-seven quid in his pocket." And he thrust an empty palm toward him. After staring at it for far longer than was necessary, Simian decided that the only way to make him, and the palm, go away was to put thirty-seven quid in it.

"Keep the change," Simian said as Colin headed back toward the bar. And then to Artemis and Poseidon he said, "It's funny because I gave him the exact money."

Neither of the gods laughed.

24

Kelly DePayne had seen some awful things during her time as an undercover agent. It was disgusting how they treated cod at Harry Ramsden's. Not only that, but she had stumbled upon evidence of an offshore account, too. And although, she had to cede, it was probably the best place to have an account if your main trade is in saltwater snacks, she had her suspicions that someone in the chip-shop trade was up to no good.

But that would all have to wait for now, as there were more important things to deal with. A good place to start would be the six dead goons strewn all around Spinelli's club.

"Any of them him?"

DePayne turned to find her superintendent, Alec Smythe, marching toward her across the dancefloor. He would have looked quite intimidating had it not been for the green and red lasers dancing all around him.

"I don't think so," DePayne said.

"In that case," Smythe said, "we have to assume he's

at large."

Stellar policework, DePayne thought. It was no wonder the people of London had lost faith in the system, with numpties like Smythe running the show. "We did find something interesting though," she said, leading Smythe across the dancefloor and out through a back door.

"It's raining out here," Smythe said, which was, DePayne thought, two out of two for the superintendent. "What's this all about, DePayne?"

"There," she said, pointing toward the thing she had brought Smythe out here to see.

"Is that... is that a whacking great big pile of horseshit?"

DePayne had to hand it to the guy. He was damn good at his job. "It's fresh, too. Forensics have given it a thorough sifting, and are confident it fell from a horse's arse at precisely the same time as those men in there were murdered."

Smythe shrugged.

"We have reason to believe that the person responsible for killing Spinelli's men escaped on horseback." Even though there were hundreds of far less conspicuous ways to flee a crime scene; she still hadn't figured out the ins and outs of it.

Smythe went back into the club, marched across the dancefloor, and arrived at the goon pinned to Spinelli's office door. "What's this?" he said, pointing up at the golden spear. "It looks like a spear painted gold." He turned to DePayne. "Is it a spear painted gold, and if it is, why?"

"This is where things start getting a bit weird," DePayne said, although after last night's encounter with a squall, and then with Simian Knight P.I. showing up to interrogate her earlier today, weird seemed to be the norm. In fact, the norm was so scarce right now that it would be weird for something normal to happen. Or something. "It might look like a spear that's been painted gold," she went on, "but it's not."

"What are you babbling on about," Smythe said, fingering the golden spear. "Of *course* it is."

DePayne shook her head. "It's not painted," she said. "That spear is 24 Karat all the way through, which would make it worth, according to today's rate, somewhere in the region of five-hundred grand, give or take a nickel."

Smythe wasn't having any of it. DePayne could see he wasn't having any of it by the way he said, "Get the fuck out of here, and don't come back until you've seen the psych nurse."

"I didn't believe it, either," she said. "I mean, why would Spinelli kill all these men, his own men, and then leave behind something as valuable as this."

"Probably wasn't room for it on the horse," Smythe said, and DePayne couldn't tell whether he was being serious or not.

"This," she motioned to the golden spear, "and the fact that these men were loyal to Spinelli through thick and thin, leads me to believe that a third party is responsible for this mess."

"And that third party is all over the footage you got from the hidden cameras in here, right?" DePayne said. "We can pick them up, charge them, thank them for taking out the trash for us, and then stuff them away in a prison for a hundred years. My god, DePayne, you're good at your job. When the Queen's Police Medal judges come around, I'll be sure to mention your name."

"Well," DePayne said, "I wouldn't get too excited. Our cameras seemed to malfunction at around the same time all this went down. We've got some lovely shots of the aftermath, though, which—"

"Jesus Christ!" Smythe said. "So far all we have is a massive pile of horseshit and a golden spear."

"We have one more thing," DePayne said. She eased Spinelli's office door open and walked through it. Smythe followed, which was good as that was what she wanted him to do. "The phone," she said, pointing down at it. "Forensics say it was used after Spinelli's men were killed, which means someone placed a call."

"And how," Smythe said, "do forensics know something like that. This isn't CSI, for crying out loud. We don't have access to all that made-up technology. This is London. We have handcuffs and aubergines. If you're lucky, you get a taser—"

"Phone records," DePayne said, holding up a sheet of paper.

"Oh," said Smythe. "Well, that makes more sense."

"At 12:48 this afternoon, Jack Spinelli put in several calls. We don't know what was said, because not only did our cameras start malfunctioning but also our concealed microphone, and by that I mean the one I popped into Spinelli's backside while he was sleeping." She shuddered. "But what we *do* know is who he called." She held the sheet out for Smythe, and he took it.

"Domino's Pizza?" he said.

"Underneath that," DePayne replied.

Smythe's eyes suddenly widened. "I'll be damned," he said.

"Probably," DePayne said, "but keep on going, it gets worse."

"The Kay twins, Frankie 'The Goon' Vermicelli, Paulie Pagoda, Johnny 'Three Tits' Maroni... why would he call all these... I don't..."

"I think," DePayne said, "we'll find out soon enough. Something big is about to go down, and this—" she motioned to the goon pinned to the door "—is just the beginning."

In real life, sentences such as this are seldom

punctuated by the actual thing being talked about happening. It would require a coincidence of ginormous proportions. A reputable bookmaker would snap your hand off if you were to walk up to the counter with it scribbled down on one of their little forms, because the odds of it actually happening are so long that you'd be better off sticking your money on a one-legged horse in the Grand National.

But this particular sentence was punctuated with an almighty bang, proving the impossible possible and causing at least two-hundred old people—all fitted with a Dodge & E. Pacemaker—to drop down dead where they stood.

"What the hell was that?" Smythe said, rushing across to the window, where he saw nothing because the window looked out onto a wall and not much else.

DePayne said, "It sounded like an explosion," because it had, and she wasn't the undercover cop she was today simply because of her cracking good looks and ability to keep a secret. "Come on. Let's go find out." She was, however, known for talking in clichés from time to time.

*

Simian passed a drinks order forward—two pints of beer and three fingers of scotch—and was pleasantly surprised when two thirds of the order came back correct. Unfortunately, his was the third that Colin had bolloxed up.

"I thought gumshoes drank hard whisky," Poseidon said as Simian set the drinks down on the tabled and fell, disappointedly, into his chair. "That looks an awful lot like a Slippery Nipple."

"I believe it is," Simian said, unable to believe his luck.

"And how would you know what a Slippery Nipple looks like?" Artemis asked Poseidon.

"I'm a regular at The Ulysses and Duck," he told her, sipping the froth from the top of his beer. "Nobody makes a Slippery Nipple quite like Costas."

"Well, whatever it is," Simian said, picking it up, knocking it back in one, and then grimacing almost immediately after, "it's gone now."

"I would have swapped with you," Poseidon said.

Simian grimaced. "A little late for that now, I should

imagine," he said. "Although there's a good chance it will be making a reappearance at some point."

Poseidon shook his head. "I'm all right, thanks."

They sat for a while without speaking; the constant chatter all around them seemed to blend into one voice. When Simian could stand it no longer, he said, "What's life like on Mount Olympus? I mean, it must be nice walking into a pub and getting exactly what you ordered."

"It's not all shits and giggles," Artemis said. "Being a god has its perks, so long as you enjoy grapes, but for the non-gods up there, I should imagine it's pretty much the same as it is here." She turned a beermat over in her hand, and then again, as if she might have missed something crucial the first time around. "I thought it would be different down here," she said, morosely.

"I *told* you what it was like," Poseidon said. "But what would I know? I'm just an old fool with a big fork and a white beard and bladder problems."

"Yes, you were right," Artemis said. "It's been fun while it lasted, but I'm ready to go home now."

"I, on the other hand," Simian said, "have to try to figure out where this month's rent is coming from." A natural disaster would, he thought, be most welcome right now. But things like that don't happen when you want them to, which was why it came as something of a surprise when the front of the pub suddenly exploded.

And things went quickly downhill from there.

25

Debris and dust rained down on the street. People screamed and ran for their lives, but since none of them had any idea which was the safest direction to run in, a lot of them ended up back where they started.

"Woo-hoo!" a voice cheered, and deep beneath the rubble of what had once been a perfectly filthy British pub, Simian Knight's ears pricked up.

For the cheer had sounded a lot like Jack Spinelli, if Spinelli had stopped being serious long enough to start enjoying life.

"You okay?" a voice said. It was Artemis, and she was lying next to him. Other than looking slightly dustier for wear, she appeared to be uninjured.

Simian pushed bricks off his body. "I think so," he said. "Although I'm not a doctor. There's a very good chance I'm dead right now. But, as I said, I'm not really qualified to make that sort of diagnosis."

All around the pub—which was now only three-quarters of a pub, and the worst three quarters, at that—there were grunts and groans as maimed drunkards emerged from the wreckage. Colin the barman stood atop an upturned fruit machine, scratching his head and, for the damn thing had started working for the first time in ten years. Cheery chirps emanated from the box beneath him, and continued to do so until he gave it a good kick and said, "My pub! My bloody pub!"

Poseidon, who had been helping people from the rubble, came across to where Simian and Artemis were dusting themselves down. "It would appear," he said, as calm as you like, "that there has been some sort of explosion."

Simian turned to the great big hole in the front of the building. "As a private investigator," he said, "I concur." Because he did.

"Come out, come out, wherever you are!" The jaunty voice was coming from the street outside, which was no longer outside because the pub was now outside, and so if they were both outside then what constituted as inside anymore? It was something that would plague Simian Knight for years to come, provided, of course, he survived the next ten minutes.

"Spinelli," Simian said.

"Who?" Artemis pulled a beermat from her ear, though quite how it got in there was anyone's guess.

"The mobster from last night," Simian said. "The one whose hand you put an arrow through."

Artemis threw up her hands. "Well, this is just getting ridiculous," she said. "You humans seem to be hellbent on murdering one another. It's a wonder you've managed to get this far as a species. I've been here less than twenty-four hours and—"

Just then there came a second voice. A great big booming voice that seemed to reach Simian's ears in 5.1 Dolby Digital Surround Sound[1]. "Could any Greek gods currently frequenting what remains of this charming inner-city public house please exit through the massive hole in the front of the building. Thank you."

Artemis and Poseidon looked at one another. It was a look that said, *Well, I never expected that!*

"Friend of yours?" Simian asked.

---

[1] Other home theatre audio technologies are available, although they're not as good and, frankly, a lot of them are like listening to film through a pair of foam-covered 1980's earphones.

"It can't be," Artemis said. "Zeus would never allow it."

"Allow what?" Simian said, stepping from one piece of broken pub to another.

"I'm going to count to ten," said the booming voice. "I'm also going to do it very quickly, because I'm rather impatient and, well, I can do what the hell I want. I am a god, after all." And the voice proceeded to count very quickly from ten down to one, which, Simian thought, was not what the voice had threatened to do, at all.

"Wait here," Artemis told Simian.

Poseidon grabbed her by the arm just as she was about to launch herself toward the opening. "He's too strong!" he said. "He'll kill everyone here, everyone in the city! Leave him to me"

"Is anyone else getting sick of the pronoun game?" Simian said, to which a hundred injured dipsomaniacs said, *Yes, yes we are, thank you very much.*

"Someone has to stop him!" Artemis screeched, shrugging Poseidon's hand off. "What's the first rule of God Club?"

"We're not to interfere with the day-to-day actions

of the human race," Poseidon said.

"I'm just shocked there's such a thing as God Club," Simian said. What's the second rule of God Club? No one is to touch Thor's hammer but Thor, because you know how pissy he gets—

"That's Norse mythology," Artemis said.

"Really?" Simian said. "I thought it was Marvel. And also, did you just read my mind?"

"I'm a goddess," she replied. "There are a lot of thing I can do that you wouldn't understand. Best not to get into it while there's a mad god out there, tearing the place up, though."

Fair enough, Simian thought.

"Good," Artemis said.

Poseidon picked up his big fork and bounded toward the opening at the front of the pub, where he stopped, looked out, seemingly surveyed the sky for a moment, and went no further. "Um," he said, lowering his trident. "I might have been a little hasty when I said I could do this on my own."

Artemis turned to Simian and said, "I'm going to tell you to stay put, and you're going to say okay, but then you're going to follow me over there anyway, because you've watched *Die Hard*[1] one too many times and you've always fancied yourself a hero and this is your chance, so why don't we skip all that and get a wriggle on?"

Wow! Simian thought. "Actually," he said, "I've always wanted to drive Jessica Tandy around in a 1949 Hudson Commodore 8, but this is the next best thing."

He followed Artemis across to where Poseidon stood, being careful not to trip on the debris and occasionally apologising to the people still trapped underneath it, for they were very squeaky.

"Should I strip down to my vest?" he asked Artemis on the way over.

"If it makes you feel better," she replied.

Simian thought about it, but then decided it was a bit nippy. Also, it was still raining outside, therefore he'd be much better off keeping as many clothes on as possible. And anyway, he wasn't Bruce Willis, this wasn't Nakatomi Plaza, and Professor Snape was not

---

[1] Simian Knight's favourite film by a country mile. His second favourite film is *Driving Miss Daisy*.

holding people hostage over the Christmas holiday, of all times.

Simian drew to a halt next to Poseidon. Artemis did the same, but on the other side. It was all about symmetry, you see. And when Simian looked out, saw the heavily armoured man sitting atop a horse fifty-feet away, and then the six mobsters floating about the sky above him like seagulls in Armani suits, he said, "Oh," which was nothing like the correct response. Most people would have said, "Bugger me!" or words to that effect, but not Simian Knight, not in that moment.

"This is bad," Poseidon said.

"Are you flexing your muscles?" Artemis asked him. "Because it looks like you're flexing your muscles."

"Am not," Poseidon replied, his muscles deflating somewhat. "I'm merely trying to figure out how we're going to come out of this in one piece."

"That's easy," Artemis said, swinging her bow around and nocking an arrow. "We're probably not."

"At least you guys are immortal," Simian said. "I'm human, and therefore susceptible to death. In fact, I'm having second thoughts about the whole thing. Perhaps I should just let you get on with—"

"That's the prick who was hiding in the bushes taking pictures," Spinelli said, looping the loop and then just hovering there like an angry hummingbird. "That lousy sock-sucker's fricking mine!" He flew forward at such speed that the resultant sonic boom shattered the windows of a tanning salon (There She Glows), a barbershop (British Hairways) and a laptop repair centre (Bits and PCs).

Sensing imminent death, Simian dove to the right, which was a mistake as that was where Poseidon was standing. He bounced off the god, and landed with a thump somewhere back in the pub. Poseidon, meanwhile, swung his trident. There was an almighty *thonk!*, followed immediately by a pained groan, and then, if Simian's ears weren't deceiving him, the comical *Wheeeeee!* of a mob boss disappearing into the distance at pace.

Post-haste, Simian got back to his feet and scrabbled across to Artemis. "How am I doing?" he said.

"Honestly?" she said, pulling back her bow. "You've lasted a lot longer than I thought you would." She released the arrow, and through the air it went, its target sitting atop a horse looking smug as hell. Well, Simian thought, he wouldn't be looking smug in a second when the arrow—

The god caught the arrow.

"Was that supposed to happen?" Simian asked as Artemis nocked a second arrow.

"Yes," she said. "That was my practise arrow."

"You're making that up, aren't you?"

"Yes."

Poseidon walked calmly forward. "You can't do this, Ares," he said. "The first rule of God club—"

"Hogwash!" Ares said. For a god, he sure did have a funny way with words. "These people are not our equals, they don't deserve all this—" he waved the caught arrow through the air "freedom. You know as well as I do, Poseidon, that they take it for granted. It would be far better if they were reminded how easily it can all be taken away from them."

Artemis fired the second arrow, and this time Ares

swatted it away as if it were a minor annoyance.

"I'm running out of arrows," Artemis said.

Simian peered into her quiver. "Doesn't that thing, like, reload automatically, or something?" he said.

She looked up at him as if he'd just asked her why a fly without wings isn't called a walk. "Do you have any idea how much golden arrows cost per unit?"

Simian shook his head. "Why don't you just paint regular arrows?" This was starting to get silly.

The god, Ares, dismounted his horse and began walking toward Poseidon, who was still walking toward Ares, who was... they would meet in the middle, at any rate.

"Can Poseidon beat him?" Simian asked, picking up a broken chair leg just in case Spinelli came back in Poseidon's absence.

Artemis nocked a third arrow, aimed it up at one of the flying mobsters, and released it. It thumped into the mobster's chest, knocking him back a foot or so, but he simply pulled it out and tossed it aside. "It's not just Ares we have to worry about," she said. "He's made these arseholes immortal."

Clutching the chair leg tight, Simian said, "That's not good," before adding, "Hang on a minute. You have the power to make people immortal? Why am I standing here like a tit in the breeze, holding a piece of the furniture and staring death in the face, if you can give me eternal life?"

"It's not as easy as that," Artemis said, and now she had a golden dagger in her hand. Lord knows where she pulled it from. "Actually, scratch that. It's pretty easy, but we don't do it because humans are not meant to live forever."

"What about Keith Richards?"

"Who?"

"The Rolling Stones?"

"Oh, that's nothing to do with us. He's been bathing in vinegar for centuries."

The sound of gold upon gold distracted Simian for a moment. He glanced across to find Poseidon and Ares engaged in battle. Only either they were both amazing warriors, which was why their strikes were always deflected by the other, or they were both really shitty warriors, for the very same reason.

The flying mobsters were getting into some sort of formation. Spinelli had returned, which was, Simian thought, testament to the robustness of his face. A golden trident would have at least left a mark, but apparently not.

"Quick!" Simian said. "You have to make me immortal."

Artemis sighed and sheathed her dagger. "If I do," she said, "will you stop going on about it?"

"No," Simian said. "But I won't mention it for the duration of this battle."

"Fine." She moved behind Simian, reached up and placed both hands on his shoulders. Simian was all at once aware of a strange tickling sensation, not unlike the build-up to a violent sneeze, and then her hands were gone, and he felt strangely violated. "It is done," she said, pulling her dagger once again. She smiled. "Go get 'em, tiger."

What followed would have caused Stan Lee to shit in his shorts, for Simian leapt into the air and, at the point when he should have come back down, all laws of physics went out the window and he carried on up.

Up, up, all the way up, screaming a war-cry, "Reeeeeeeee!" and hoping he didn't collide with any overhead wires before he reached Jack Spinelli and his band of immortal mobsters.

"Reeeeee!"

26

DePayne and Smythe ran along the street, which took them forever since everyone else was running in the opposite direction. It was like wading through mud, only this mud was screaming and trying to get away, therefore it was nothing like wading through mud, and whoever came up with such a ridiculous comparison deserves to be fired, or shot, or both.

"Look!" Smythe said as they finally made it past all the screaming humans. "It's chaos! It's madness!"

DePayne saw the decimated pub first, but then her eyes were pulled inexorably toward an ongoing battle in the middle of the street between what looked like God and a Spartan. The *chink* of big fork upon golden sword was deafening. She instantly recognised the old man from the previous night, for he was wearing sandals and DePayne never forgot a funny shoe. "That's him!" she screeched over the clamour. "That's the guy who showed up last night while I was meeting Spinelli!"

Smythe's frown slipped down one side of his face. "What are you talking about?" he said. He was about to add to that when something swooped down from the sky, latched onto him, and pulled him unceremoniously away from the earth.

"Smythe!" DePayne screeched, and tried to sound like she actually cared. She looked up, watched as one of the Kay twins—Bobby or Billy, she wasn't sure which—soared through the air, her superintendent holding on for dear life and screaming like a cornered frog.

Producing a loudhailer, for she always kept one about her person, she said, "Let go of him right this minute." Then she realised what she'd said and decided to clarify. "That is, fly him down here and place him carefully down, or so help me God…"

She tailed off there, for that was when she noticed Simian Knight P.I. up there in the sky, whirling round and round with Jack Spinelli as if auditioning for some sort of ridiculous dancing show. She scratched her head, came over all nauseated, then staggered back, for she was clearly going insane.

That was when a body fell from the sky and landed with a crash upon the roof of an unfortunately placed

Datsun Cherry. Its windows exploded outward, and the car lost several inches in height in less than a second. "Damn, that hurt!" said the Girl Guide as she rolled off the crushed classic. When she saw DePayne standing there, she said, "Hey, you're the lady from last night. Glad to see you've still got your head. Does he always kiss like that, or—"

The girl did not get the chance to finish her question as Frankie 'The Goon' Vermicelli landed next to her and punched her across the street, where she proceeded to slide down a lamp-post with all the grace of a reversing dump truck.

Vermicelli shook his hand out, the way people do after they've punched someone into the future.

"Freeze, Vermicelli!" DePayne said, thrusting the loudhailer toward him and then remembering, far too late, that it wasn't a gun.

"You must be Margot," Vermicelli said, jiving toward her like a pound-stretcher version of Frank Sinatra. "Spinelli told me all about you," he went on. "But what he forgot to tell me was how beautiful you are."

"Charm ain't talking you out of this one," she said. "On the ground! Now!" She wished she'd brought her aubergine with her. Or at least a pair of handcuffs.

"Hey," Vermicelli said, coolly, "maybe we can talk about this back at my place. I'm a god now. A nice broad like you and a god like me, we could make some cute half-god babies, capeesh?"

"You're not a god," DePayne said. "You're a freak of nature. An aberration. And also you smell."

The grin dropped from Vermicelli's face like an anvil. "You know," he said, "you try to pay a broad a compliment these days, and that's the thanks you get." His eyes suddenly glowed red and his teeth, DePayne noticed, grew an inch in his mouth. Sharp they were, too. Like alabaster stalagmites. "I'm a firm believer," he said, although it was a bit of a struggle since he quite clearly hadn't got used to his new teeth, "in treat 'em mean, keep 'em keen."

"That's funny," DePayne said. "I'm a firm believer in once an arsehole, always an arsehole." She brought the loudhailer up and yelled into it. "Stop! Stop! He's going to kill me!"

Her reasons for doing so were twofold: firstly, there was a very good chance that she was telling the truth, and secondly, to put into motion the events that followed.

"Shut up your whining," Vermicelli said. His glowing red eyes were, DePayne thought, awfully off-putting. "Ain't nobody gonna save you."

No sooner had the words passed his lips than Jack Spinelli landed on the ground between DePayne and Vermicelli, cracking the concrete in the process. He turned to Vermicelli and grunted. It was the kind of grunt that DePayne would have found charming, under other circumstances, but this wasn't other circumstances, and so it came off as a little annoying.

"Jack!" Vermicelli said, sucking his teeth back in. "You're just in time. I was about to tear this pig limb from limb."

"You'll do nothing of the fricking sort," Spinelli said. "Remember that redhead I told you about? Well this is her. I almost didn't recognise her with the megaphone." He turned to DePayne. "What's with the police gear, sugarcube?"

"First of all, don't call me that. I am not, have never been, and will never be your sugarcube."

Spinelli looked a little taken aback. "Um," he said. "Whatever, honeybunch."

"Secondly," she went on, "I'm here to arrest you, Spinelli. I've been undercover this entire time."

"But," he said, and then said it three more times just to make sure. "I was going to leave my wife for you."

"No you weren't," DePayne said.

"No, you're right," Spinelli said. "Oh well, this is all a bit of a turn up, isn't it?"

"You've been cosying up to some cop, Jack?" Vermicelli said.

Spinelli turned on Vermicelli. "You shut your fricking mouth, Frankie. In fact, let me help you with that." He raised his hand, which no longer bore any signs of the wound from the previous night, and waved it once from right to left. Vermicelli gasped, staggered back a few steps, fell on his arse, got to his feet, and then felt around the bit of his head which used to be his mouth. There was no sign of it; DePayne was just as shocked as Vermicelli.

"Mmm!" said the panicked gangster. "Mmm-mmm-mmm!" Then he leapt into the air and kept on going.

Spinelli turned to DePayne and grinned. "You double-crossed me," he said. "And nobody double-crosses Jack Spinelli."

"I hate it when people talk about themselves in the third person," DePayne said, moving slowly away from him. "Sure, it's fine if you're famous. You can get away with it. But a nobody like you? It just sounds pathetic." Her whole life had started to flash before her eyes, which is never a good sign.

Here she was at the academy, running through the woods, climbing over perfectly-placed obstacles. "That's not one of my memories," she said. "That's the beginning of *Silence of the Lambs*."

"Who are you talking to?" Spinelli said. "And stop it."

DePayne thought about screaming for help. She also wondered where Superintendent Smythe had got to. The riddle was solved less than ten seconds later when he landed with a meaty thump on the pavement to her right.

"Friend of yours?" Spinelli said. "You'll have to forgive my boys. We're all a bit new to this godly powers and immortality palaver. I'm sure we'll get better with practice," he snorted, "and let's just say, we have all the time in the world to practice."

This was all getting too much for DePayne. She preferred it when things had been simple, when gangsters didn't fly through the air like skylarks and the only men in the city on horseback were made of stone and wore a traffic cone on their bonce. Suddenly the world had gone crazy, and she didn't like it one bit.

"Spinelli!"

DePayne looked to the sky, as did Spinelli. "This mangy sock-sucker again," he sneered.

But DePayne just watched, mesmerised as Simian Knight, the world's least busy private investigator, singlehandedly battered the Kay twins before turning his attention back to Spinelli.

"Why don't you come up here and take on someone your own size?" Simian said. Vermicelli flew toward him, but then dropped out of the sky as a golden arrow thunked into the side of his head.

"I'll be right up," said Spinelli, before turning to DePayne and adding, "We'll talk about this later." He kicked off the ground, and for a moment DePayne's hair and clothes tried to follow him. She was extremely glad when they didn't.

And then all she could do was watch as the madness continued to unfold all around her.

27

"Spinelli!" Simian said, though as soon as the gangster turned and looked up at him, he wishd he hadn't bothered. *I'm not a superhero!* the voice in his head said, and it was a voice he trusted implicitly. Then Billy and Bobby Kay, London's most feared twins— although all twins are creepy, and should be treated as such—swam through the air toward him. One of them appeared to be swinging a sock with something heavy in it, while the other was in the process of rolling his suit sleeves up in preparation of a bout of good old-fashioned fisticuffs.

Hit the smallest one first! the trustworthy voice in his head said. So Simian did as he was told. It wasn't until much later that he remembered that the Kay twins were identical, and therefore neither was the smallest one. If anything, they were both the biggest. But, as his mother used to say, "The bigger they are, the harder they fall," and while Simian had never seen the sense in such nonsense, he was surprised by how hard Billy and Bobby Kay fell from the sky when he hit them.

He looked back down at Spinelli.

"Why don't you come up here and take on someone your own size," he said, to which the voice in his head said, *Look, if you're going to keep digging yourself in deeper, don't come crying to me when you're all twisted up like last year's Christmas lights.*

The next thing Simian knew, he was violently dancing with the gangster again. "This could go on for some time," he said, dodging a right hook that, had it connected, would have sent him back in time.

"Getting tired already?" Spinelli said, parrying a foot.

"I could do this all day," Simian said, although he rather hoped he would not have to. People were watching, and there were sirens in the distance, although it sounded as if they were going in the opposite direction.

"Me too," Spinelli said, before adding, "you sock-sucker!"

It transpired that Simian didn't have to worry about fighting all day, for in the next second he was flat on his back, staring up at the sky and wondering how the cheeky bastard had managed to sneak a jab through.

*

Artemis soared across the road like a penguin on steroids. Ares, who had been busy fending off Poseidon's trident, was not prepared for her. She landed on his back and instantly wrapped her arms around his head.

"Shit!" he said, for she had covered his eyes and was trying to twist the whole thing off. "Gnh!"

"I can't hold him all day!" she screeched to Poseidon, who had suddenly frozen, as if unsure what to do next.

Artemis didn't have a clue, either. In fact, she felt silly now, her little twelve-year-old legs swinging around as Ares tried to throw her off. Lord knows what she looked like to an innocent bystander.

A dick, probably.

"Stab him in the neck!" Poseidon said. "Or anywhere! You know how much he hates pain!"

She released Ares with her dagger arm and arced it down in a perfect semi-circle. Any watching mathematicians would have swooned, but unfortunately all the mathematicians had scarpered at the first sign of trouble.

The golden dagger stuck in Ares' chest, and he said, "Arghyerbastard!" which was the perfect response for a dagger to the sternum. "Oh, it hurts! It hurts so much! Pull it out! Actually, don't pull it out! You'll only make it worse!"

Artemis slid off Ares' back and landed on the ground, which would have been fine had there not been someone there already.

"...offa me!" said the body beneath her.

"Offa him!" said another body. This one was upright and marginally angrier than the one beneath her, although they both looked the same.

"Argh!" Ares groaned as he staggered back and forth, always arriving back at the same spot. "Make it stop! The pain is too much!"

Artemis climbed off the complaining body. "You two must be twins," she said, in that way people so often do when they are faced with two indistinguishable humans. "Which of you is the oldest? I'll bet it's you, isn't it?" She pointed at one of them, though which one she couldn't tell as they were so alike.

"We're the Kay twins," one of them said. "Notorious twins of the East End, and—"

And that was as far as he got before Artemis drop-kicked him into oblivion.

"Hey!" said the other one.

"Oh, come on," Artemis said, "He was asking for it." And this one, she thought, is too, but before she could do anything about it, Ares bounced into her, knocking her back.

"I'm blind!" Ares cried. "From all the pain!"

"Artemis!" Poseidon said. "Hold onto something." She grabbed onto Ares, and Poseidon went on, "Hold onto something that isn't about to be blown to kingdom come."

Fortunately for Artemis, there was a lamppost not three feet away, and she lunged for it just as Poseidon's eyes rolled up into his skull.

The storm came a second later.

*

"Having a bit of a stinker, aren't you?"

It was, Simian saw looming over him, the delectable redhead. "You could say that," Simian told her. "I always thought immortality and superpowers would make me happier, but so far it's caused me nothing but pain."

She helped him to his feet, which was good as that's where he wanted to be. "You're one of them, too?" She motioned to Poseidon and Ares, and then to Artemis, who for some strange reason had wrapped herself around a lamppost.

"Not quite the same," Simian said, because he wasn't. He was still, and would always be no matter how many powers they gave him, human. You could polish a turd, but at the end of the day it would still be a turd. In fact, it would be a turd all through the day, just slightly shinier.

A peal of thunder suddenly echoed all around the sky. It was so loud, and so sudden, that Simian almost swallowed his tongue. Fortunately, his tonsils had been in the way.

"Not *this* again," said the redhead.

"Poseidon's summoning a storm. Find something

to hold on to," Simian said, and then, "No, not me! Something fixed firmly to the ground."

She raced across the street, and Simian followed her, to where a graffitied post-box stood. It was a special post-box, inasmuch as there was a piece of paper Sellotaped over the bit where the letters go in. Written on it in thick, black marker were the words OUT OF ORDER DUE TO NESTING BADGERS.

"Hold tight!" Simian said just as a bolt of lightning split the sky in half.

"What about the badgers!" asked the redhead.

"Screw the badgers!" Simian said, wrapping his arms around the post-box and interlinking his fingers. It hadn't occurred to him that badgers were far too big to fit in the post-box, which was just as well as he had enough on his plate.

The wind picked up as a low pressure surged through the street. Coupled with a high pressure coming the other way, it really was the perfect storm. The only thing missing was George Clooney.

Simian closed his eyes.

Now that he was immortal, there was no need for

his life to flash before him, which was a shame as it would have given something to concentrate on as all around him the world fell apart.

*

Poseidon concentrated. So hard that he almost gave himself a hernia. A fork of lightning stretched down from the sky and struck the tines of his trident, fizzled for a bit, and then dissipated like a fart in a hurricane. The sky grew darker, and darker, until it was almost impossible to see the street around them. Confused birds flew up into their trees and tucked themselves in for the night. A familiar looking fox wandered nonchalantly out onto the street, saw the chaos, and then decided to pop off somewhere else, somewhere less... fighty.

"Last chance, Ares!" Poseidon said, his voice barely audible over the clamour of the storm. "Rescind the immortality spell on these men and return to Olympus."

"What?" Ares said, still clutching at the dagger sticking out of his chest.

"I said," Poseidon said, a little louder, "make these

mobsters mortal again and piss off back to the mountain."

"I will do nothing of the sort," Ares said, drawing his back-up sword[1] from its holster. "This is your last chance to join me, Poseidon, for there is no Mount Olympus, not anymore."

Poseidon dodged a flying car, then swatted a motorcycle and its courier aside as it came at him, carried on the wind. "What have you done?" Poseidon asked, for he knew the glint in Ares' eye, had seen it upon many occasions, and it never failed to cause his hackles to rise.

"The palace," Ares said through gritted teeth, "is in the void. I have no home to return to, and neither do you." He yanked Artemis's dagger from his shoulder and hissed like a deflating balloon. "It's over, Poseidon. And now I will rule over this world, the way we always should have, and neither you nor Artemis can stop

---

[1] As well as his primary sword, Ares carries a back-up sword, six daggers, a catapult, a flamethrower, two pairs of nunchaku, a frisbee, and a spikey ball on a bit of chain. He lives by the rule: Better to have it and not need it than need it and not have it. Apart from the frisbee; that's just for fun.

me." He took out his frisbee and, with a flick of the wrist, sent it toward Poseidon, who watched as it fell quite a way short of the mark. "Damned frisbee!" he said.

Poseidon roared and began making his way toward Ares. Mobsters came at him from all sides, but Poseidon sent them back into the sky with a swing of his trident, where they were buffeted about on the strengthening tempest.

Ares stood his ground, dug his sandals in, and prepared for the final showdown. God versus god. Earth was their boxing ring now, and one of them was going to lose. The trick was making sure it was the other god.

There came a thunderous boom, a flash of lightning, and something else that sounded a lot like, "Bugger! Overshot my landing!" Poseidon turned and stared into the dark miasma that now enveloped the street. The storm abated, for Poseidon had to be completely focused in order to channel the weather, and the truth of the matter was the thunderous boom and the flash of lightning had nothing to do with him, which meant—

"Everyone!" said the voice. "Don't panic! Zeus is here!" And then Zeus appeared at the end of the street, thunderbolt in hand and a wry grin stretching from one side of his beard to the other. "Ah, there you are." He stagger-walked toward Poseidon. "Glad to see you've got things under control here. Might I suggest turning the storm down a little bit. I can hardly hear myself think."

"Zeus!" Poseidon said, and sure enough the thunder and lightning ceased, and the wind dropped a couple of notches, too.

"Zeus?" Ares said as he took several steps away from the King of the Gods. "How? It's not possible."

"Not possible?" Zeus said. "Ah, you mean my being here. Yes, it was awfully inconvenient floating about in the void for almost ten whole minutes, but you'd be surprised how easy it was to get out of." He stroked his beard, ran his fingers through his long white hair, and said, "Oh, I almost forgot—" he waved his thunderbolt through the air, and then it rained mobsters for a moment. They picked themselves up, and considered making a run for it, and would have, had it not been for the black-and-whites howling onto the street from all directions, their lights flashing, which generally meant they weren't pissing about.

"Good to see you, Father," Artemis said, sidling up next to Zeus. "I'm sorry. I should never have come to Earth. It was a mistake, although I did have this really nice breakfast. I had to go to the toilet—"

"We can talk about it when we get back," Zeus said, although his tone suggested he would rather not. "Ares, you betrayed me, you placed your entire family in jeopardy, and you almost started World War III. Do you have anything to say for yourself before I mete out your punishment?"

Ares dropped to his knees and sighed. "Do what you will," he said, lowering his head. He had a terrible off-centre bald spot. Poseidon thought about mentioning it, but then decided there were more important matters at hand.

"Ares, God of War," Zeus said, "I hereby sentence you to two weeks of hard laundry. You will hand in all weaponry upon our return to Olympus, and will only get it back when I'm confident you're not going to use it for nefarious purposes." He paused for a second before continuing. "You will no longer have access to FaceSpace, and I expect you to clean your room thoroughly, or so help me, Me, I will turn you into a goblin, paint your toenails red, and turf you out onto the street with a sandwich board offering free hugs to all non-gods. Have I made myself perfectly clear?"

"Yes, Father," Ares said, lifting his head a little. He wore the sad expression of an admonished pug. It was not a good look for him.

"Right, that's *that* sorted, then," Zeus said. "Better be off—"

"Wait!"

Zeus turned and frowned as a dishevelled man approached. "Did you just say 'wait'?" he asked.

"I did," said the man. "That is, if it's not too much trouble."

Zeus was about to tell him that, yes, he had better things to be doing than waiting, and that he would rather be off doing them right now, thank you very much, when Artemis said, "Father, this is Simian

Knight. He investigates privates for a living."

"Actually," Simian said. "That's not what I do at all." He shot her a reproachful look, not that it made the slightest bit of difference. To Zeus, he said, "I just wanted to say that you were the best thing about *Percy Jackson and the Olympians*. Reckon Sean Bean had you down to a tee. Of course, it's one of only a handful of movies in which he didn't die, which is testament to your—"

"You're babbling, Simian," Artemis said.

Zeus simply smiled, for he wasn't sure what else to do.

"We have to go now," Artemis said. "But be sure to not mention this to anyone ever."

"Mention what?" Simian said, and then they both went, "Aaaaah!" because it was so damned clever. "No, but really, I'm already traumatised to the point of putting the whole nasty affair out of mind, lest I wind up in a loony-bin, screaming into the night until someone comes with a syringe to silence me."

"Good for you!" Poseidon said, whacking Simian playfully in the arse with his trident.

"Why is that woman beating those poor men with an aubergine?" Zeus asked no one in particular.

"Long story," Artemis said, "but I believe she is an 'under the covers' cop, and those men are criminals of the highest order."

They all watched as Jack Spinelli and his crew were loaded into paddy wagons. Then the men in blue began walking toward where they were gathered at the end of the street. "You'd better go," Simian said. "The last thing you need is a trip down to the station. Trust me, it's unpleasant. Lots of awkward silences and interview-room shenanigans. They'll have a field day with you lot, dressed like that. Just go. I'll explain things."

"You're a good man, Simian Knight," Poseidon said. "But a terrible gumshoe."

"Beats being unemployed," Simian said, but only to himself, for Zeus, Poseidon, Artemis, Ares, and the jet-black horse which had been parked at the side of the road, were all gone. It was as if they had never been there to begin with[1].

---

[1] Or something less cliché.

"What the hell just happened?" asked one of the approaching officers.

"Where did those idiots in fancy dress get to?" asked another, staring blankly up into the clearing sky.

"Who?" Simian said, turning this way and that for dramatic effect. "What idiots? What fancy dress?" It was best, he thought, to play dumb. Fortunately, he was rather good at it. Very little effort required.

Once the officers were satisfied that they were all suffering some kind of group hallucination, they returned to their vehicles and peeled out of the street, sirens blaring and tyres squealing. It was all, Simian thought, completely unnecessary, but then he put himself in their shoes and arrived at the conclusion he would have done exactly the same.

Now that the gods were gone, Simian felt a little bit lonely. He'd rather enjoyed his little tête-à-tête with Artemis and Poseidon. It wasn't every day you got to hang with the gods.

He crossed the street and headed toward what was left of The Fox. Colin was standing in the new open-plan drinking area, surveying the damage with his wonky eyes.

"Simian?"

It was the redhead, Margot Trix or whatever her real name was. "I didn't see anything," he told her. "That is, I haven't a clue what just happened and I'd rather not think about it."

"I just wanted to thank you," she said, rubbing at her neck. "Whatever happened here today, it wouldn't have happened without your help."

Simian didn't know quite how to take that. There was appreciation in there somewhere; he just didn't have the energy to go looking for it. "You got your man," he said, pausing at the entrance to the pub.

"The next time Jack Spinelli tastes freedom," she said, "we'll all be hovering around in flying cars and having sex with robots."

"At the same time?" Simian asked, for an image appeared in his head and he didn't know what else to do with it. "A bit dangerous, that, don't you think?"

The redhead laughed. She laughed and laughed until, Simian thought, it started to sound a little sarcastic. After far too long, she said, "Where are you going?" for Simian had turned to make his way into the broken pub.

"There is," Simian said, "a golden arrow sticking in the dartboard, and I'd hate for someone to take advantage of it."

28

He'd just lit a cigarette and poured himself half-a-pint of whiskey when there came, upon his office door, a rather trepidatious knock. Simian stared at the door and the door stared back. After several more seconds of this, he waved his hand through the air and the door flew open, crashed against the back wall, and slammed shut again. It all happened so fast he didn't get a good look at his caller.

"Shit," he grunted. He hadn't quite grasped his new powers yet. In fact, so far, the only use he'd made of them was when the toilet was backed up yesterday. He'd cleared that mess in no time, just by looking at it and focussing. If there had been anyone present, they would have thought him mad, but Simian Knight was not mad. He was, apparently, the log whisperer.

"Come in," Simian said to the silhouette.

"What was all that about?" asked the dame as she came through the door.

"Oh, *that!*" Simian said. "Yes, there's an awful draught in here. Doesn't know whether it's coming or going." He looked at the beautiful blonde the way a hungry man might look at a steak menu. "Please, take a seat, tell me what I can do for you."

The dame sat, lit a cigarette, then threw one leg over the other and relaxed back in the chair. "You're Simian Knight," she said. "*The* Simian Knight."

"It was the sign on the door, wasn't it?" Simian said. "Whiskey?"

"No thanks. I had a Tizer before I came out." She looked at Simian the way a hungry woman might look at a paddling pool filled with roadkill. Simian didn't know whether to take that as a compliment. In the end, he decided to ignore it. "I hear you've recently had… an encounter."

"I've had *lots* of encounters lately," Simian said with a smile. At least, he thought it was a smile, but he had been wrong before. And also, he was suddenly very aware at how that came out. *Blondes, brunettes, redheads, an endless stream of beautiful dames. The queue starts over there, if you want to find out what real disappointment feels like.* "I mean, I have no idea what you're getting at." Of course he did. She had to be referring to the gods. But how did she know? Who had been talking? And why?

The dame crushed out her cigarette in the overspilling ashtray on the desk. "You're a funny little man, Mr Knight," she said. "At least, I'm sure some people think so."

"Yes," Simian said. "I mean, not really. Some people think I'm an arsehole, but—"

"I have a job for you, Mr Knight. A very important job, with very little remuneration."

"Sounds right up my street," Simian said. "I take cheques that will most likely bounce, Scottish banknotes, and, if it's a really tricky job, I wouldn't say no to a nice piece of haddock."

The dame nodded. "I'm sure we can come to some sort of agreement." She reached into her clutch and came out with what appeared to be a receipt. It was, like most receipts, crumpled up. "I'm afraid it's been through the washer several times."

"That's receipts for you," Simian said, accepting it from her and examining it closely. He uhhmed and ahhed for a bit, just so it looked like he knew what he was doing, and after a while he said, "Am I right in deducing the item described on this tatty piece of paper is missing, presumed stolen?"

"You really *are* good," said the dame.

"Hm," Simian said. "Well, I will need a retainer," he went on, "just to pay for filthy motels, whiskey, expensive meals in restaurants that allow you to smash the plates, and suchlike."

"Anything you need, Mr Knight," she said, marginally more excited than she had been before. "So, you'll do it? You'll go to Greece and find it for me?"

Simian smiled as he stood, pulled himself into his trench-coat, popped his fedora on, and knocked back his whiskey in one huge gulp. Once the unbearable burn in his stomach and throat faded, he said. "I'm already on it."

"Oh, Mr Knight! You have no idea how much I appreciate this. That golden fleece is a family heirloom, you see. Belonged to my great, great, great, great, great, great, great—"

"Is this going to take long?" Simian said, lighting a cigarette and ushering the dame out of his office so he could lock up. "I've got a plane to catch."

"Did you know," said the dame, "you've got a massive burn-hole in your carpet?"

Simian sighed. "I did," he said, turning the key in the lock. Another reason for taking up the hunt for the misappropriated golden fleece was that he would be out when the carpet-fitters came tomorrow, with their hammers and Stanley knives and incessant demands for tea and biscuits.

He was rather looking forward to the case ahead. It would be nice, he thought, to take on a job that had nothing, nothing at all, to do with Greek gods.

"What's your name, by the way?" Simian asked as he led the dame down the stairs and out onto the street. "I like to know who I'm working for."

"My name?" she said. "Of course. I'm Medea, daughter of King Aeëtes of Colchis. My husband, Jason—"

"That's quite enough!" Simian said, turning around and heading back up the stairs. Medea looked shocked, and also flabbergasted, but she did not follow him, which was probably for the best.

Back in his office, Simian locked the door and

lowered the Venetian blinds. Tomorrow he would nip the golden arrow down to the pawnbrokers, see what the mean old bastards would offer him[1]. For now, he was quite content to stand at his window, the slats of the Venetian blinds playing about his face as he sipped whiskey and smoked cigarettes.

That was what being a P.I. was all about.

And Simian Knight had it down to a tee.

---

[1] Five grand and anything he fancied from the VHS shelf, including the XXX stuff.

Printed in Great Britain
by Amazon